HORIZON DELTA

PRAISE FOR HORIZON ALPHA: PREDATORS OF EDEN

"A heart-pounding adventure. . . . It's *The Walking Dead*, but with dinosaurs. Like a hungry T-rex, *Horizon Alpha: Predators of Eden* got its claws right into me." —**Gillian Philip, author of the *Rebel Angels Series***

"I've often dreamt of trying to survive on a new planet and pitting myself against nature. My dreams were never this chilling, nor the ending as thrilling. I highly recommend this high energy adventure and would place it between Isaac Asimov and Arthur C. Clarke." —**Reid Minnich, author of the *Koinobi Trilogy***

"There's plenty of jet fuel for the imagination. The pace is fast, the stakes are high, and the safety of no one is guaranteed." —**John Burris, author of *Brothers***

PRAISE FOR HORIZON ALPHA: TRANSPORT SEVENTEEN

"*Horizon Alpha* is a melting pot of all my favorite things: far-out sci-fi, gripping survival horror, and best of all, friggin' dinosaurs!" —**Tony Moore, Artist of *The Walking Dead, Fear Agent, & Deadpool***

"A rollicking adventure for sci-fi and dinosaur fans." —**Mike Fredericks, Editor, *The Prehistoric Times***

Books and Series Featuring D. W. Vogel

HORIZON ARC

Horizon Alpha: Predators of Eden

Horizon Alpha: Transport Seventeen

Horizon Alpha: Homecoming

Horizon Alpha: High Wire
A Short Story

Horizon Beta

Horizon Delta

Super Dungeon Series

The King's Summons
by Adam Glendon Sidwell and Zachary James

The Forgotten King
by D. W. Vogel

The Glauerdoom Moor
by David J. West

The Dungeons of Arcadia
by Dan Allen

The Midnight Queen
by Christopher Keene

HORIZON DELTA

Horizon Arc book 5

D. W. VOGEL

FHP

Horizon Delta

Future House Publishing

ISBN: 978-1-950020-03-4
ISBN: 978-1-950020-08-9 (ebook)

Developmental editing by Emma Heggem
Substantive editing by Stephanie Cullen
Copy editing by Olivia Chantry and Abigail Miner
Interior design by Kate Staker
Proofreading by Abby Siebers

This one's for my doctors. You're building the bridge I'm walking on.

CHAPTER 1

I always knew I'd never set foot on a real planet.

My destiny was in the stars.

The Horizon Delta left Earth over two hundred years ago, bound for Chara d. It was a generational ship, hastily built as one of four arcs to carry humans across the galaxy, away from an Earth that only had a few years left before Mercury crashed into it. My parents were born on the Delta. My grandparents were born on the Delta. And if things had gone according to plan, my children and my children's children and another two hundred years' worth of my descendants would be born on the Delta before it finally reached its intended destination. That far-off future child would walk on a planet's surface . . . assuming the star called Chara had a habitable planet when the Delta arrived. Those long-dead Earth scientists had more hope than knowledge, but then, hope was really all there was in those dire days.

Things apparently went pretty well for the first hundred years of the Delta's trip. By the time I was born, fifteen years ago, things weren't going nearly as well. Of the three great spinning cylinders that gave us our artificial gravity, only one was still spinning. The rest had gone still, and our people had moved everything critical into the aftmost cylinder. We still thought we'd make it.

When I was twelve, the propulsion system failed. The Delta was dead in space, drifting on its trajectory, slowing every hour.

When I was fourteen, life support failed in the dead cylinders.

And on my fifteenth birthday, a meteor struck the ship.

My four-year-old brother's sprained wrist saved both of our lives that day.

He came running into the medical bay just as I was cleaning up. Doc Walsh had started my medical apprenticeship, and I couldn't wait to start using all the things I was learning. So when Shane came in crying, cradling a swollen wrist with his other arm, I knew just what to do.

"Doc, it's Shane," I called. "He's hurt."

I helped my brother hop up onto the exam table and wiped his eyes and nose. His face was red from crying.

"So what happened, buddy?" I asked. "Did you fall?"

He shook his head. "I was just playing. Too much gravity."

Each ring of the great spinning cylinder we lived in had different levels of gravitational pull provided by centrifugal force. The ones in the center had the least, and those around the outside, including the med bay, had the most. It was easy to misjudge your footing, especially when moving from one level to another.

"Okay, you'll be all right. Did you call for Mom and Dad?"

He nodded. "They're coming."

I started to pull the machine out from the wall to take an X-ray of Shane's arm. "Let's just get a picture and make sure nothing's broken."

The floor vibrated once under my feet, quick and sharp.

Three seconds later, the entire ship rocked with a jolt that knocked me to the floor.

Shane gripped on to the exam table, wide-eyed. "What was that?"

Warning sirens wailed through the ship, and the robotic voice we'd come to fear blared through the comm system. "Emergency. Emergency. Hull Breach Alert. Proceed to the nearest . . ."

The voice stopped.

The sirens stopped.

Distant sounds of metal on metal screeched through the med bay.

"Jonah? Is it a drill?"

I shushed my little brother, holding my breath to listen. The floor shuddered under my feet again. Not a drill.

"Off the table," I said, slinging an arm around Shane's waist and swinging him to the floor. "Stick close to me, whatever happens. Do you hear me?"

Shane gripped on to my leg with his good arm, and I grabbed his face between my hands, forcing him to look into my eyes.

"Hear me? No matter what, you stay right next to me."

He nodded, lips starting to tremble.

Doc Walsh appeared from another room, followed by Marie, his nurse.

"Come with me right now," he said, voice deceptively calm. Anyone who didn't know him wouldn't realize he was on the verge of panic. But I had been working with him for a year. My heart pounded and my mouth went dry. This was bad. Very bad.

I shouted as we ran out of med bay and into the corridor. "What's happened? What's going on?"

He grabbed Shane by the bad arm and pulled us down the hall. Shane squealed and jerked away. Doc didn't even glance down, eyes darting into each connecting hall that dead-ended into ours. I gripped onto Shane's good arm and followed my mentor, heart pounding.

This is bad. Worse than bad.

The overhead lights winked out, replaced by a glowing green chase of emergency lights along the floor.

"Hull breach," he panted as we ran. "Emergency doors are closing, but if it's a big enough hole, they won't hold. Not for long."

We stumbled in the dim light, feeling the ship creak and buck beneath us. The carpet under our feet was worn to almost nothing after generations in space. I knew every bare spot, every dent and ding in the walls. The deep, low rumbling of humanity's ark had been background noise to my entire life. But today the sounds were alien to my ears. The normal, smooth motion of our cylinder hitched, and the distant screeches of metal on metal sounded like screams.

Shane was crying again. "Where's Mom? Where's Dad?"

I had no answer. "Just stick with me, buddy. It will be okay. They'll find us."

The hallway ended at the entrance to one of our shuttles. In the far-off future when Horizon Delta finally arrived at its destination, those shuttles were meant to take our descendants down to the surface of a new planet.

The four of us piled into the shuttle. About a dozen other people were already inside, shouting and climbing over each other to make room.

Another huge bang rocked the ship.

I was born on the Horizon Delta. I knew the emergency drills. In case of a hull breach, get to a shuttle. All along the ship were emergency doors designed to slam closed and restore the pressure in the undamaged parts of a breached cylinder, but the shuttles were the safest places with the strongest doors, designed to survive entry into a planet's atmosphere.

Those huge bangs had to be the interior emergency doors giving way, one by one. In a matter of minutes, the entire ship would lose pressure and atmosphere. Anyone not in a shuttle would die in the freezing, airless dark.

Dark shapes stumbled toward us, holding onto the walls as the ship vibrated.

"Here! Here!" I yelled. "Get in here, fast!"

Shane was at my hip and I pushed him behind me. "Get back, buddy. Stay inside with Marie. We have to get people in and get the door shut before . . ."

I didn't say before what.

People pushed in past me, and I squinted down the hall.

Mom worked in engineering and Dad would have been working on dinner prep in the kitchens. Neither location was anywhere near us. But still I hoped.

"Come on, Mom. Hurry, Dad."

Another bang. Louder.

Two more people pounded down the hall, yelling as they came.

"It's all going out. The whole ship. No pressure . . ."

I could just see the emergency door at the far end of the corridor sealing this section of the cylinder off from the rest of the ship. As I watched in horror, a tiny crack appeared around the edge.

"Run!" I screamed at the people.

But the crack widened. Our air pressure rushed toward it, dragging the people backwards, away from where I was standing.

My feet flew out from under me as the leaking pressure pulled me toward that door, but strong hands grabbed my arm and pulled me back into the shuttle's open doorway.

"Get clear," Doc yelled, and I braced myself against the inner wall of the shuttle.

The people in the corridor were scrambling against the pressure. I couldn't tell who they were, but they weren't my parents.

"There are still people out there! We can't close it—" I began, but the crack in the emergency door widened.

"Back!"

The shuttle door slammed down, sealing us inside.

Through the thick metal, I heard the last emergency door give way.

I rushed to the back of the shuttle, peering into the darkness behind the ship. A stream of debris floated away from the Delta. Everything that had been inside was being forced out into the vacuum of space.

Everything. Everyone.

Shane crawled up next to me, and I turned him away from the window.

"Don't look, buddy. Just don't look."

HORIZON DELTA

We sank to the floor of the shuttle as the dreams of Horizon Delta floated away in the icy emptiness behind us.

CHAPTER 2

Thirty of us had managed to claw our way to one of the shuttles attached to the outside of our drifting ship. The auxiliary power inside still worked. We had air to breathe, and the pressure held.

As the damaged cylinder stopped rotating, we lost our gravity. Over what must have been about ten minutes but felt like eternity, we got lighter and lighter until the cylinder ground to a halt. Everyone that wasn't strapped in began drifting around the cramped interior, pulling themselves along from seat to seat, hand over hand. Shane and I stayed buckled in, ducking as people and debris banged around our heads. I had always enjoyed traveling to the center of the Delta, where I could float and bounce down the core of the ship. It never upset my stomach like it did so many others. But now my stomach churned, and the back of my throat tasted like the algae I'd eaten for breakfast. My heart was light in my chest—not from joy, but from the lack of gravity pulling it down. My sinuses felt stuffy.

And of course, none of that mattered.

Thirty people were crammed into a tiny shuttle meant to carry our descendants down from the orbiting Delta to a new planet. It wasn't packed with food. We had a couple of bottles of water bouncing around with us. The power might last a month, but we'd starve to death much sooner.

Intellectually I knew all this. But my brain was still in shock, reeling from the terror of those last moments before the hatch slammed shut.

I hadn't even begun to process the loss of my parents and all my friends. Sooner or later it would hit me, but for now, the only thing I could focus on was keeping my brother alive. Keeping him from falling apart in the hopeless few days before we joined our parents in the stars. Shane was all I had.

Doc Walsh tried to keep our spirits up.

He floated at the front of the shuttle's open cockpit and put on a brave face. "I know this looks bad," he said, and we waited to hear the "but" we hoped would follow. "It looks very bad. But we're alive, and where there's life, there's hope."

Oh boy. Relying on old clichés. Life and hope. That was the best he could do.

"What hope?" The voice from the back sounded like we all felt. Like the speaker was wishing this were all a horrible dream and he'd wake up back on the Delta heading for Chara d.

I wrapped my arm around Shane's shoulder and gave him a little squeeze. He was being so brave, never complaining though his wrist was still swollen and painful.

Doc Walsh gave a little smile. "I don't know what hope. But we're here. We're still here. And I guess that's all we have." He sank back into the cockpit.

My little brother piped up from beside me. "Maybe someone will rescue us."

Everyone turned to look at him, but no one bothered to answer. In two hundred years of travel, the Delta had never encountered any other spaceships. The Horizon Alpha, one of our sister arks, should have landed by now on the other side of the galaxy, and the Beta would still be underway toward Omicron Eridani. Neither was heading in remotely the same direction as we were. And as much as I wanted to believe there were friendly aliens zipping around, the chances of any of them stumbling across our dead, drifting ship were basically zero, if they existed at all.

I strapped myself in and threw an arm around Shane. "Maybe someone will."

And if they didn't, we'd all starve in the shuttle, or die of dehydration when the water ran out.

Oh, Shane. I would do anything to spare you that fate. But there was nothing I could do. Nothing any of us could do but wait in the tiny shuttle. Wait to die, like everyone else we'd ever known. I made up stories to keep him amused but struggled to think of happy endings.

We talked about freeing the shuttle from the side of the Delta and trying to fly it somewhere. But we were light years from any known planetary system. The shuttle would never make it anywhere near a star. We stayed attached to our mothership, hoping against hope that if anyone was looking, the Delta made the biggest target.

There were whispers around the cabin that we should just open the hatch. Make it quick, instead of suffering. When we started to die off, we'd be stuck in the shuttle with the dead. Someone would be the last to go. The last person alive from the great Horizon Delta, doomed like the Earth we came from. People muttered about opening that hatch and popping out into the vacuum. Quick, but not painless. People whispered about it, but nobody was brave enough to reach for the hatch control.

We made it three days.

I was dozing when Shane nudged my arm. It was nearly impossible to sleep without gravity, with only the shuttle's seatbelt preventing me from bouncing around the cabin. My stomach had given up growling and the shuttle reeked of frightened people with no toilet facility. The grumblings about opening the hatch were getting louder. It was the day the water would run out, and we'd eaten nothing for seventy-two hours.

"Jonah?" Shane nudged me again. "Jonah, you awake?"

I muttered and opened my eyes.

He was looking out the window at the black sky full of stars.

"Try and sleep, buddy," I said, and turned away from him.

"No, Jonah, you have to look. I saw something."

He's getting delirious. Little kids can't go very long without food.

"It's nothing. Just close your eyes."

He punched me in the shoulder. "Look out there."

The punch didn't hurt. Without gravity, he couldn't get much force. I looked out the tiny porthole, following his pointing finger.

"There's nothing there, buddy. Just black sky."

He nodded. "Yeah. No stars. And the no stars are moving."

It was such an odd thing to say that I made the effort to focus my eyes. Doc Walsh had started teaching me about medicine. I was going to be the ship's next doctor before we lost propulsion. He insisted I start learning anyway, and I humored him even though we had all known for the past year that we were never going to make it. One of the things I learned was that human eyes had evolved for gravity, and in a no-gravity environment, they swelled up. It's why they had built the med bay on the outer edge of the cylinder, where gravity was strongest. More gravity helped people heal faster.

The stars out the window were blurry, and I squinted to see where Shane was pointing.

Black sky, just like all the black sky around it.

But as I watched, a star winked on right in the middle of the sky. Another blinked off. My heart pounded in my ears as I watched. It was a black, empty space in the sky, and it was moving. Stars in the front went out, and stars behind flicked back on.

I had no depth perception. It could have been tiny and close, or far away and huge.

But the longer I watched, the surer I became.

Something was out there. Something black, blocking the stars as it moved across the sky.

And it was heading straight for us.

CHAPTER 3

Other people noticed the black spot in the sky. Murmuring broke out all through the shuttle, and the people on the side that was attached to the Delta left their portholes, which showed nothing but Delta's metal hull. They pulled themselves over to peer out the windows on our side.

"Something's there. Something's coming!"

It felt stupid to hope after we had all given up. But as the black hole got closer, it reflected the few lights that still shone out from our shuttle.

It wasn't a hole.

It was a ship.

Huge, black, and smooth, it came into focus like a shiny, dark bean in the sky, reflecting off the few lights that still shone from the dead Horizon.

"Rescue! Someone's coming for us!"

Nobody even asked who it was. The giant black bean wasn't the Alpha or the Beta. It wasn't anything a human had ever seen before.

Aliens. It was a spaceship made by aliens. And it was coming right at us.

It lumbered right past our windows, close enough that we got a good look at its side. No windows. No steel plates. Just a smooth, unbroken hull of reflective darkness.

"Who is it? What do they want?" The murmuring grew into shouts. "Do they know we're in here? Flash the lights!"

Nobody paused to wonder if the aliens would be friendly. We were starving. Doomed. No matter who they were, being found was surely better than dying one by one in the filthy shuttle.

The giant ship cruised past as Doc hurried up to the cockpit to flash the cabin lights on and off. It was a waste of our precious little power, but no one complained.

The ship didn't slow down.

"Where is it? What's it doing?" Shane pressed his face against the thick glass.

The bean disappeared from our view. Doc Walsh yelled back from the cockpit. "I think it's turning. It looks like . . ." He paused for a moment. "It looks like it's attaching itself to the front of our ship."

"Our shuttle?" I asked. I hadn't felt a thing if the giant bean had made contact.

"No, the Delta. It's kind of . . . sucked on to the aft cylinder."

Our shuttle rattled then, and we all gripped onto whatever was closest. Someone was floating right above my head, hanging upside down, trying to get her face in next to

Shane's at the window. When the shuttle vibrated, she kneed me in the face.

"Hey, watch out." I glared up at Marie, the nurse from sick bay. "Oh, sorry."

She didn't even answer. Everyone was looking around in shock.

This was it. Aliens. Real aliens, here to rescue us.

"I can't believe it," Marie said from above me. "We're saved. We're really saved. How lucky can we get?"

She was grinning, and I looked around the dark shuttle. Everyone had crazy smiles pasted on their faces. *Rescued. We're rescued.*

"What if they don't come get us?" Shane gave voice to the doubts I was feeling.

What if they don't? I unbuckled my seat belt and pushed away from the seat, heading for the crowd trying to cram into the cockpit. *What if they do?*

Noises echoed from the other side of the hatch that connected us to the mother ship.

"Everybody shut up!" I yelled, stopping my forward motion and pressing my ear up against the cold metal. "They're on the other side!"

Icy fear shot through me. If they opened the hatch from their side, we'd all die. The Delta's life support was gone. Everything in the back third of the ship would have been sucked out the hole by now. The aliens must have space suits to survive with no atmosphere.

Or they don't need space suits. Or oxygen. Or any of the things we need to live.

"Hey, don't open the hatch!" I yelled into the steel hull. *Genius. They're sure to speak English.*

They didn't open the hatch.

Right in front of my eyes, a tiny spark lit up. I jerked my head back as the spark grew into a fiery glow no larger than my finger.

"They're making a hole in the hatch!" I whipped my head around. "Get me something to plug it so we don't lose air!"

A man behind me ripped his shirt off and stuffed it into my hand. I held it close to the bright circle on the hatch, ready to stuff it in as soon as the hole opened.

The bright glow died, and when I could bear to look straight at it again, there was no open hole. Instead, a dark green tube poked straight into our shuttle. It looked like a long finger with no joints, just a waving tube of green.

Like a plant. A vine.

It pushed itself into the shuttle just past my face and I shoved myself back, bouncing off whoever had pressed in behind me. No one spoke. We watched in wonder as the little tendril waved around for a few long seconds.

It retreated, and I reached out with the shirt to plug the hole it was going to leave behind. But it left no hole. When the questing green "finger" disappeared, it was instantly replaced by a thick green plug, neatly filling the tiny hole.

I heaved a sigh.

"They know we're in here. They know we need air to breathe." I hoped my words were true. But what had that odd green finger been attached to? Who were "they"?

The sounds on the other side of the hatch faded off into the distance.

Marie grabbed my arm from behind. "Are they leaving? They can't leave us!" She pounded on the hatch, yelling, "Come back! Come get us! Don't leave us here!" Everyone else joined her, beating on the side of our shuttle that abutted the Delta's dead hull. If the green-finger aliens were coming back, there was no way we would hear them.

"Everybody be quiet!" Doc's voice thundered from the cockpit. "The ship is coming back!"

The huge black bean appeared in the outside windows. The smooth, shiny hull made it almost impossible to focus on, but the dark hole in the stars got bigger and bigger.

Shane grabbed my hand and whispered, "They're going to squish us."

And it looked like he was right. The ship got closer and closer until it was pressed right up against our window. If the thick glass hadn't been there, I could have reached out and touched it. What would it feel like? Soft? Slippery? Cold?

The blackness outside the window was complete.

"Why is it just sitting on top of us?" I wondered aloud.

Another voice from the other side of the ship was laced with panic. "It's all around us! It's between us and the Delta!"

I pushed back to the Delta side of the shuttle. The blackness oozed around those windows, filling in the gaps between us and our mother ship. I whipped my head around in time to see a faint yellow light opening up on the other side.

"It's all around the ship. It's absorbed us inside it! It's swallowing our whole ship!"

There was nothing to see in the yellow light on the far side—just a pale glow. My eyes still couldn't judge distance, but I thought there might be . . . a wall? Was our whole shuttle inside some kind of chamber in the black bean ship?

Gravity snapped on. All of us who had been floating around above the shuttle's seats crashed to the floor. My chin bounced off the armrest, and someone landed right on top of me. The cabin filled with groans and whimpers.

I staggered to my feet and looked from side to side. On the Delta side, the bright light fired out the windows nearest the closed hatch that attached us to the Delta. It spread all around until I had to avert my eyes.

What's happening?

With a crashing jolt, the fire disappeared. The yellow glow wrapped around all sides of our shuttle.

Doc's voice from the cockpit was full of wonder.

"They've cut us away from the Delta without breaching our hull. We're inside their ship. Our whole shuttle is inside their ship."

The yellow glow dimmed. Walls. There were definitely walls out there. Doc was right. Our shuttle was sitting on the floor of some kind of huge hangar. The distant walls were bare and green, or maybe blue reflecting the yellow light that had no apparent source. Through the tiny window by my brother's face, I could see the edge of something made of dark metal. It was angular and large, but I couldn't see the whole thing.

Our hatch was locked with a thick metal wheel. It gave a great screech and slowly began to turn.

I grabbed Shane's arm. "Stay close to me. Whatever happens, stay with me."

They're opening the hatch. I watched, mesmerized, as the gray wheel spun. *What if there's no air in their ship? What if there's no pressure?*

The hatch swung open.

CHAPTER 4

In the old books and movies we had brought with us from Earth, people always imagined aliens from Mars. They were often described as "little green men" and usually didn't come in friendship and peace.

The creatures that waited outside the hatch door were little and green.

But they most assuredly weren't men.

Maybe eight of them stood back from the hatch. No two looked quite alike. Ranging in color from a pale yellow-green down to an almost black blue-green, they had limbs numbering from four to six, except one that appeared to have at least ten. None of them were more than waist-high to me. Their skin was mostly smooth and shiny, though some had wicked spikes protruding from their backs and arms. Most of them were standing on two legs, in roughly human form, though a couple were decidedly not humanoid in shape. The ones without obvious heads were just hard to look at, and I wasn't sure if they were looking back at us or not. A couple carried items that must certainly be weapons—hard, rounded things made of some kind of solid, plastic-like material.

There were eyes trained on us. Generally two per alien, except in the case of the many-legged fellow, who was also similarly blessed in the eye department. I decided to call him "Spider," no matter what his actual name turned out to be.

Doc Walsh stepped forward. With an embarrassed, nervous look, he gave the traditional Earth human greeting when faced with a group of aliens.

"We come in peace. Take us to your leader."

The aliens scuttled back at his words. Weapons were raised.

They huddled together for a moment, appearing to communicate in some way, though none of them made a sound. After a few tense seconds, they broke apart and made an aisle down the middle of their group.

Do they want us to walk through there? What do we do?

None of us had any idea how to respond. My feet were rooted to the floor of the shuttle, hands gripping Shane's arm hard enough that he'd probably be bruised later. I wanted to relax my grip, but my hands wouldn't respond.

Aliens. Actual aliens. On a huge black spaceship that had just swallowed our shuttle and cut it away from the Delta. We were standing in artificial gravity on an alien spaceship. Maybe rescued from certain death.

Maybe heading for something even worse.

Warm, humid air wafted into our shuttle from their ship. I inhaled, bracing for toxic gas or sickening fumes, but it smelled thick and clean. Anything would smell cleaner than the inside of our shuttle.

Doc tried again.

"Does anyone speak English?"

Of course it was a ridiculous question. English died two hundred years ago when Earth was destroyed. But what else could he say?

The tallest alien, an algae-green one that walked on two legs and carried one of the weapons, strode toward us. He was the most humanoid in appearance, with two eyes in roughly the correct place. He had no nose and no mouth but did have what might be some kind of ear hole on each side of his head. His feet were wide and flat, like lily pads on a pond.

I looked at the rest of the aliens. They all had feet like that, of varying numbers.

I decided to call this tall one "Eddie" because in my whirling, panicked brain, that struck me as hilarious.

Eddie marched straight toward us, and we parted to let him pass. He moved into the shuttle and around behind us and started pushing us toward the open hatch.

"Do we go out?" Doc's face was full of wonder.

What choice did we have?

We filed out of the shuttle between the columns of waiting aliens. None of them had made any noise beyond the sticky, sucking sound it made when they picked up their feet off the floor of the hangar.

They ushered us around the front of our shuttle, and I got a first look at the inside of their ship.

My eyes were still swollen from the days of no gravity, and I squinted to focus. The hangar we were in was enormous. Our shuttle sat just behind me, and across the room was another metal-hulled spaceship a bit larger than ours. It was basically tubular in shape, with a large, open hatch on its side. It had symbols painted behind the hatch that must have been writing in whatever language these creatures used to communicate.

Behind that ship I could just make out a different shape that was probably a third metal shuttle of some kind.

The floor and walls of the hangar were a mottled blue-green, lit by a soft yellow glow that seemed to emanate from every surface. There were no obvious light sources on the walls or the smooth, unbroken ceiling high above us. I turned to look back at our ship and saw that these aliens had cut through the wall of the Delta that had attached the two-sided hatchway to our shuttle.

They knew we couldn't survive in a vacuum. They kept our hatch intact until we were safely on board their ship.

Did that mean they were friendly?

Shane asked what I was thinking. What we all must have been thinking.

"Who are they? Are they friendly?"

I pulled him closer to me and whispered, "I don't know. I think so. They saved all our lives."

If only they'd arrived a few days earlier. My heart gave a squeeze. *Mom and Dad.* And everyone else. *Best not to start down that road.* I'd avoided letting myself think about our parents since the horrible moment that the Delta's hull was breached. *Don't go there now. You'll never come back. Shane needs you.*

The aliens marched us between the pockmarked shuttles that looked so different from the interior of the black bean ship that held us all. Were those the shuttles of other rescued space travelers? Were these little green guys some kind of cosmic lifeguards, scouting the galaxy for disabled spacecraft and saving the survivors of interstellar disasters?

HORIZON DELTA

I looked in vain for any more of our shuttles in the hangar. Surely other people had managed to evacuate in time. But if they had, the aliens hadn't rescued them. Ours was the only Horizon shuttle in the ship. Our little group of survivors were the only ones here.

Across the hangar, other green aliens were moving equipment into a long hallway. I recognized things from the Delta: parts of the command bridge, computers, some of our entertainment systems, and a large, covered, rolling bin of the algae that was our staple food. It must have been strapped down when the hull breached and sucked everything out of the ship.

They made a bucket brigade, passing items from our ship along their alien chain to who-knew-where. I watched them move crates of our seeds, meant to plant on the new home we would never reach. A giant cooler full of animal embryos took six of them to slide along. Wouldn't do them any good. All those systems lost power years ago. Nothing was still viable in that cooler.

A poke in the back of my thigh jerked me back to focus. Shane and I were last in line, and the rest of our people were exiting the hangar, escorted by more of the small green aliens.

"Where are they taking us?" Shane gripped my hand, shuffling along beside me.

"I don't know, buddy. But it has to be better than the shuttle." At least it smelled better.

They took us down a long hallway, featureless blue with the same yellow glow. We huddled together as we moved deeper into their ship. My hair was sticky with perspiration in the close humidity.

Doc's voice echoed down the hall. "Are you taking us to someone who can talk to us?"

The aliens didn't answer.

The hallway let out into a wider corridor. At long intervals, closed hatchways lined the hall. From behind some of them came the sounds of moving creatures, with strange bellows and cries.

Ahead, the crowd of humans stopped. I pulled Shane ahead of me and stood blocking him from the aliens behind us. "Whatever happens, stay with me," I whispered.

One of the aliens touched a small plate outside the hatch. It opened, and the front half of our group was ushered inside. Doc Walsh, at the head of the group, was held back by two of the aliens holding his legs. One of them looked like it would be slippery to touch, like an eel. In the dampness of their ship, I wondered if they came from a water planet. Did they live in giant pools somewhere in this ship and only come onto dry land to rescue doomed ships floating in space?

The hatch closed, and the remaining twelve of us trooped farther down the hall, along with Doc.

Another hatch was opened.

As the rest of our people were herded through, Shane and I passed Doc, still being held by the aliens. I paused next to him.

"Are they taking you to the leader?"

He nodded. "I'm sure they are. They obviously think I'm in charge of us, so I'm sure they're going to try and figure out how we can communicate." He smiled. "Don't worry, Jonah. I'll find a way. We'll all be fine."

Eddie, the light green spaceman, poked me in the thigh again, and I followed Shane into the room beyond the hatchway.

It closed behind us, and the humans were alone once again.

CHAPTER 5

We lost all sense of time.

Counting me and Shane, we were twelve people. Marie was part of our group, along with Mr. Khatri, one of Shane's teachers. One of my mom's friends, Mrs. Carlotti, was there, but neither her husband nor her daughter had made it out. Mr. Conrad was our math teacher, and Mrs. Lucien worked in the kitchen with my dad. I was the youngest, next to Shane. My mind skittered away from the thought that every one of our friends, every kid on the Delta except us, was gone.

The room we had been sequestered in was almost as featureless as the rest of the ship we had seen. No windows. A long trough on one wall. Just the door through which we had entered, with the panel on one side that didn't respond to our touch. Flat, clean, and mottled blue-green with streaks of black, lit by the yellow glow that had no obvious source.

Well, at least it started out clean.

Nothing in the room appeared to be a toilet of any kind, so we picked a corner and kept the mess confined. The first time the aliens came back, they brought a large, black machine of some kind that vacuumed up the mess. Later, they returned with a big round pot that they pushed into that corner, and we assumed it was for us to stop making messes.

The long trough filled with water through a small pore that opened intermittently in the wall above it, and we drank with our faces stuck right in the water. It tasted cleaner and fresher than anything I'd ever known in my whole life on board the Delta, and I sucked it down. When the water level got low, it refilled itself from the little spout.

Those first hours were the worst. The shock of losing everyone on the Delta was creeping in around the edges, and although we felt safer here than in the doomed shuttle, nothing our rescuers had done really made us feel safe.

There was nothing at all to do. Once we established that there was no way out of the room, no secret hatch into the ventilation system or any way to open the single door, we just sat on the floor, talking in small groups.

Shane and I stayed mostly to ourselves. I could hear the whispers of fear from the adults in the room, but they always hushed right up and pasted on smiles when Shane was in earshot, pretending an optimism that none of us felt.

Mrs. Carlotti pulled Shane onto her lap. He looked at me for rescue, but I just shrugged. She hugged him close, and I could tell she needed the hug a lot more than he did.

"I know it's scary here," she told him, "but I'm right here for you." She glanced up at me, lips trembling. "Me and Jonah, we won't let anything happen to you." I'm sure she thought it was very helpful, but we both knew that with everything that had already happened to Shane in his four short years, there wasn't a thing we could do to prevent something even worse. We couldn't have been less prepared for everything we'd been through in the last seventy-two hours.

At mealtimes, the aliens wheeled in our algae bin, a giant square container on wheels taken from the Delta. We plunged our hands in and slurped up the food. When we tried to follow them out the hatch with the bin, they pushed us back.

We were polite and obeyed. No one had to get shot with their strange guns, if that was what they were. The aliens pointed them at us as if they were guns.

And even if we left the room, where would we go? Doc Walsh hadn't come back. We hadn't heard from the other half of our group, sequestered in what must be a similar room down the hall. Sometimes we heard the faint bleating noise from whatever was behind the other hatches we had passed, but as hours blended into days with nothing to do, people started getting angry.

"They're not rescuing us. They're keeping us in here like livestock." Nurse Marie was dirty, like all of us, despite our efforts to wash up in the trough.

They gave us water in a trough. Hard to argue with her there.

"Maybe they're not set up for passengers," I said. "They can't have known they were going to find us. Maybe they're like . . . cowboys on Earth. Maybe this is some kind of cattle transport and this is the best they can do. At least they're feeding us."

Over the following days—days? weeks? We didn't know— the algae changed. They still brought it in the giant tub, but instead of a uniform green slime, it had chunks in it. They were large and soft, pale brown in color, and they tasted like nothing I'd ever known. Meaty, savory, and a little salty.

"Is this alien food?" Shane asked, scooping up some of the chunks.

I shrugged. "It's whatever they're making for us."

Mrs. Lucien, who worked with my dad in the kitchens, thought it might be some kind of bean paste. Back on the Delta, they'd had access to all kinds of cookbooks and recipes from Earth's history.

"We never had all those foods to try," she said, holding one of the chunks up to the light, "but some of the descriptions were quite vivid. I have no idea if tofu tasted like this stuff, but it sort of looks the same."

A few days later, the algae had carrots in it.

We'd grown things in the gardens on the Delta. I knew what carrots looked and tasted like. I also knew that there hadn't been anything left of our gardens on the ailing Delta for the past three years, since we had to reroute all our available power into one small area's life support. They didn't get carrots off our ship. They could have gotten seeds, but how could they have grown and harvested carrots from seed in just a couple of days? Maybe carrots were found all around the universe. Maybe these creatures had their own. They sure tasted like ours, though.

We started to count the days as three feeding times. In the never-ending yellow glow, we sat and told stories remembered from books and movies we'd known on the Delta. We argued about where the green aliens were taking us. We imagined a new planet full of the little things. Would we be welcome? Would we become kings of the mute little creatures? Everyone had opinions and guesses.

They came for Mr. Khatri after dinner.

Four of the aliens opened the hatch after the algae bin was rolled away. They didn't seem to have any particular one of us in mind. Spider was there, but not Eddie. They walked through our little group, sticky feet squeaking on the floor. I wondered if they were suction cups of some kind. Did they even need whatever kind of artificial gravity was holding us down? Surely they did, or their ship wouldn't have it. Again, I wondered if they were sea creatures of some kind.

They selected Mr. Khatri, apparently at random, and pulled him toward the hatch.

He tried to resist, but they must have been a lot stronger than they looked. None of them was anything but skinny, with spindly limbs ending in a variety of appendages. But Mr. Khatri was pulled along.

"Don't let them take me!" he cried, grabbing at the open hatchway, but none of us grabbed for him.

That still shames me.

I should have tried to hold him back.

But nothing like this had happened, and we didn't know what to do. We let them take him.

They didn't bring him back.

The next time they came in without bringing the cart, Marie stepped in front of them.

"I demand to know where our people are." Her voice shook, and so did her hands, but she folded her arms and stood up tall, looking down at the tops of their heads. At least the ones that had heads. "You're not taking anyone out of here until we know that everyone is safe and where you're taking us."

They took Marie.

This time we tried to help her, grabbing her hands as they dragged her away, but the little creatures really were strong. Stronger than us. Marie disappeared out the hatchway, and we were left behind the glowing blue door, pounding and yelling for them to bring her back.

After Marie, no one really seemed to be in charge. Ten of us were in the room, including me and Shane. None of the ship's officers had made it out. We were all just people, colonists hoping to send our children's children's children to a new planet where humans could thrive.

We sat in a circle, arguing about what to do.

Mr. Albert thought we should be patient. "There's no point fighting. They're obviously way past us, technologically." I remembered him from the ship as being constantly tidy, with a short, trimmed beard. Now he was a furry mess, and kept pulling at the long dark hairs on his chin. "They're stronger, and even though they don't seem very smart, somebody smart must be telling them what to do. We just have to wait and see where they're taking us."

I shook my head. "Assuming we're going to get there. Where did they take Doc? Where did they take Marie? Why haven't they come back? This is a livestock ship." I indicated the water trough. "They didn't even think we knew how to use a toilet. What if they're eating us, one by one?"

Mr. Albert scoffed. "You've seen too many movies. It's obvious we're intelligent. We had a spaceship, even though it didn't work. They're not eating us. They're just transporting us."

But more people seemed to agree with me. Something was very wrong here.

Next time the hatch opened, we rushed them.

The ones with the guns responded, and Mr. Albert fell, clutching his head and screaming. The rest of us jumped back, and the creatures waved the guns at us.

We didn't get our algae that meal.

They dragged Mr. Albert away and closed the hatch behind them.

And I knew I was right.

Somehow, I had to get out of this room. Had to find out what was really going on here.

And I had to do it while there were still any of us left to save.

CHAPTER 6

They brought the algae with its mysterious new additions three times a day. At least, that's what we called a day. We didn't know where they stored it between our feedings, but it was wheeled in by the little monsters in our original tank from the Delta.

The tank had a lid.

We would lift the lid and eat with our bare hands. The green slop stuck to us up to the wrists, and our water trough stayed murky green after we all washed our hands after a meal. Where we missed a spot, it crusted into a hard, flaking shell. It actually tasted pretty good once it dried. Crunchy.

I told Shane my plan and held him while he cried about it.

"Please don't go," he whimpered into my chest. "Don't leave me here alone."

My arms held him close, and I rested my chin on his head. "I wish I didn't have to, buddy. But somebody has to figure out what's going on here. Somebody has to go look for the others." And no one else was volunteering.

A few of the people tried to dissuade me, but once my mind was made up, there was no changing it. "I'm going out there. Once I see what's happening on the rest of the ship, I'll find my way back. Maybe I can get some of their guns." Visions filled my head of us storming out of this grimy hold, guns blazing to take over whatever kind of spacecraft this was. Never mind that I hadn't seen any kind of controls that a human could operate. Never mind that we had no real idea where we were in space. Never mind any of the questions and worries that raced through my mind.

We weren't livestock. And we had a right to know what was going on.

The next "morning," the aliens wheeled in the algae tank. They never stayed to watch us eat, just brought it in and left it for half an hour or so. They weren't even tall enough to remove the cover by themselves, so I wasn't worried they'd see me.

Against the wishes of half my hold-mates, and hardening my heart to my sniffling brother, I climbed into the tank.

The algae clung to every part of my skin, drenching the filthy uniform I'd been wearing since the Delta's hull gave way days ago. Days? Weeks? I wasn't even sure. But I knew I stank, despite my efforts to wash off in the water trough.

The top half of Shane's face peered over the edge. "Please don't go."

I almost didn't. Tears were welling up in his eyes. I was all he had left. But that was the point. No one was going to save us. Either I left the room like this or I left it when the little green things dragged me out. Either way, I would soon be separated from Shane.

"I have to go. But I'll come back for you. Don't ever give up hope. Promise?"

He nodded, sniffling. "Promise."

I sank down into the goo so only my nostrils and the top of my head stuck out. The others pushed the lid over my head, and I settled into darkness. Algae squelched between my fingers. The smell was overpowering in the closed tank, and my head started to ache within minutes.

In the dark, squishy pool, I waited.

The aliens never seemed very interested in us when they came in, as long as we weren't causing a ruckus. I listened to the sounds of our people moving away from the tank to huddle together in the corner, disguising the fact that they were one fewer than normal.

So many things could go wrong here.

They might realize the tank was heavier than normal. I was small for my age, but still. They might look inside. They might take it to some kind of processing area and dump the whole thing into a strainer that would chew me up without slowing down.

The hatch slid open, and I could hear the aliens scuttle in. Their feet made little noise on the smooth floor, but the tank gave a slopping lurch, splashing algae up over my head, and the bottom vibrated under me as they wheeled the tank out of our compartment.

I longed to pop my head out and look around but dared not move. There was no purchase to hold on to in the slippery tank beyond bracing my feet against the bottom sides of the slick surface. My butt slid around when the tank abruptly turned a corner, and I sank all the way under the algae's surface. I clawed my way back up and tried to wipe my eyes, but my hands were coated with the slime. I could feel chunks of carrot in my hair but couldn't risk moving around enough to dislodge them.

A hatchway hissed. Noises, feet moving on a floor.

The hatchway closed, and the lid of the tank was hauled away. I gasped for air, shoving my face up out of the tank.

A woman screamed. A human voice.

"Shhhh!" I whispered, blinking my eyes against the drippy slime. "It's me. Jonah."

"Jonah Campbell?"

Faces peered in at me from all sides, and questions peppered me.

"Where were you? Why are you in the tank? Do you have Doc Walsh with you? What about the others?"

There was no point getting out just to get in again, so I hung onto the edges of the tank and looked around at my fellow Delta survivors.

"There are ten of us now, in another room, I guess. We don't have Doc. He's not here?"

Of course he wasn't. Did I think he would be?

I told them about Maria and Mr. Albert and Mr. Khatri. They had lost two of their own, which accounted for everyone that had been on our shuttle for those awful few days.

"I'm hiding in here because somebody needs to figure out what they're doing with our people. We can't just let them treat us like this."

Heads nodded all around. "But you're just a kid," a man said. I thought it was Mr. Earle but couldn't be sure with slime caking around my eyes.

"I'm small and light," I countered. "They wheeled me in here, and they'll wheel me out. Anyone heavier and they'd notice."

"Is your brother okay?"

Shane was the youngest survivor. Thinking about him gave my heart a squeeze. *I left him. I had to.*

"He's fine. For now. But they keep taking us. Where? What are they doing with our people?"

No one knew.

They took their handfuls of lumpy algae from the edge as far from my filthy form as possible.

"Sorry, guys," I muttered. "I don't like it any better than you do." At least I got to pick some of the carrots out of my hair.

They slid the lid back on, and I hunkered down again. In a few minutes, I felt the tank bump and slosh again.

A hatchway hissed open, and when they wheeled it out, the algae splashed in the other direction. Wherever they were taking me, it wasn't back to my people's hold.

I pushed my feet against the insides of the tank and held my breath as the aliens pushed me along into the depths of their spaceship.

CHAPTER 7

I counted the seconds silently and tried to keep track of the turns that made me lose my footing and dunk back under the surface.

Twenty-five seconds. Left turn.

Forty more seconds. Left turn.

Ninety-two seconds. Ascending a ramp? The tank slowed down, and the algae sloshed in my direction. I managed to keep my face above it and breathe, but there was no hanging on as we made a right, then another left.

How will I find my way back? Assuming I got out safely. Assuming they didn't catch me.

Finally, the tank stopped. Outside its walls, I could hear a lot of the little pattering noises the aliens' feet made on the floor. Splashing water and a low, machinery hum.

The lid began to slide back, and I ducked my head under the surface, holding my breath, blind and deaf as the algae clogged my ears.

Wait. Count the seconds. Relax. They're right here.

When the need to breathe burned my lungs to failure, I pushed my face up and grabbed a huge, gulping breath.

Back under. Wait.

No one came to haul me out. No strange green tentacles probed in the algae, looking for me.

Back up and breathe.

Back under.

I did this for another ten breaths, until my head was spinning and I feared I might pass out.

Just my face out. Just until I can breathe again. Until I'm not so dizzy.

I kept my eyes closed and breathed as quietly as I could. I hoped if anyone was looking, I would just look like more lumps in the algae. My face and hair were surely caked with it.

Be still. Don't move.

When my head settled down, I risked opening my eyes.

A bright golden light burned overhead. The sides of the tank were higher than my face, so I couldn't see more than the blinding glow. I pushed my head a bit farther out. My ears were clotted with algae, but I could still hear the little feet pattering all around.

Wait. They had to sleep sometime. Surely they did.

It felt like an hour passed before I realized the sounds of feet had tapered off. I listened for long moments. Nothing.

Algae squelched out of my ears when I tried to clear them, pushing a green, slimy finger into each canal. *Not making it better.*

But the room was quiet.

I couldn't get my feet under me in the slippery tank, so I had to grasp the sides. If anyone were looking, there was no way they'd mistake me for lumpy algae.

Squinting against the harsh yellow light, I peeped my head over the side.

To my left was a blank wall. To my right, a large, open room.

Growing things were everywhere. The bright golden lights shone down on everything. Black squares of soil in raised beds nurtured long, twisting vines. Other beds held fluffy green tassels, just poking up out of the dirt. Some of the soil in other beds was almost white, with all shades of brown in between. There were hanging tubes with strange fruits dangling from holes. Water tanks sprouting brown, hairy lumps. It was a garden out of a nightmare, but as far as my green-slimed eyes could tell, nothing was moving. No aliens.

Time to move.

My legs were jelly after the slippery ride, but I hauled myself to my feet and clambered over the side of the tank. Green algae splashed around me. Should I try to clean up my footprints? I wiped at my face, but my hands were as slimy as everything else, and all I did was smear it around.

I scuttled around behind the tank and waited. If any aliens were watching, they'd surely come for me.

No one did.

The room was quiet except for the gurgling splash of moving water. I crept out from behind the tank and looked for an exit. Our people wouldn't be here in this grow-room. It was bright everywhere, and I looked for the large, square shape of the hatchway doors.

There. On the far side of the room, a hatch stood open. Lucky, because I had no idea how I'd open it if it had been closed. The aliens just touched the panels and the doors opened.

Sticking to the wall, I dashed along, crouching behind giant round, white vegetables and tall tanks of black water.

On the far side of the room, a row of long white tables stretched the length of the chamber. Each one had a trough down the middle, with little pores at regular intervals in a brown tube that ran above it.

The first trough I passed smelled like nothing I'd ever experienced. Rotten and sour, it turned my stomach. Brown liquid oozed out the pores above the trough and pooled in the long groove. I didn't pause to investigate.

The next one held a much sweeter-smelling liquid. Pale pink and opaque, it was thicker than the stinky brown stuff.

The third tube spat out little brown seeds that clinked onto the table and rolled toward the center.

The fourth trough oozed an orange liquid that smelled like . . . carrots.

I looked down the length of the groove in the smooth white table. Orange liquid filled the groove all the way down.

You're not here to learn their farming techniques.

But I had to see.

Crouching down below the level of the table, I followed it across the room. At the end, the liquid dribbled out onto a little ramp. It seemed to get thicker as it descended the ramp, and by the time it had reached floor level, the texture was thick and gelatinous, still smelling strongly of carrots.

A small cart loaded with flat, white trays sat next to the bottom of the ramp. It was full of precisely-cut squares of the orange stuff. The trays on top were still squishy. The ones on the bottom had hardened.

I took one of the squares in my green, crusty hand.

Don't do it. You don't know what it is.

I nibbled the edge.

It was carrot.

Noise behind me made me drop the rest of the chunk. I bolted down the length of the table and edged around the open hatchway door.

A long hallway was open before me. The same mottled blue-green as the rest of the ship, it seemed dim after the brightness of the grow-room. Keeping low, I crab-walked the length of it.

The far end of the hall branched, and I chose the right turn for no reason at all.

Another hallway. This one was shorter than the one before it, and I ducked under the low ceiling.

The hallway's walls ended, and I crept out onto a wide catwalk over a huge, open room below. Crouching low, I peeked over the sides.

The room was filled with long white tables, just like the grow-room. Aliens of all shapes stood at the tables, working with bits of the white plastic-looking material that the tables and weapons the aliens had used appeared to be made of. This was clearly a factory floor, and the little green creatures were hard at work building all the things that made a spaceship work. It looked like a crazy, alien version of Santa's workshop, only instead of elves making toys, this was aliens making guns. Every alien looked subtly different, though more than one had at least ten legs like the one I called Spider behind its back.

I inched farther down the catwalk. At the far end, the floor was covered in large brown mounds that appeared to come through the wall from another room beyond. At intervals along each of the mounds were small holes. The mounds had an almost woody look, like old vines looped along the floor, dotted with knotholes.

When a green alien approached one of the knotholes, it opened like a mouth. Smooth, white liquid poured out. The alien waited a moment, then picked up the gelatinous material in wide, flat hands perfect for the purpose. It carried the goop to one of the tables and began rolling it into long, flat sheets.

I stared down at the scene. The huge brown vine things were extruding the stuff they made things out of. All along the brown lengths, holes opened and more of the goo oozed out. *What a strange factory.*

At the end of the catwalk, an open hatchway gaped. Beyond was a dimly-lit, enclosed corridor that angled downward. I crept down the ramp. There was nowhere to hide. If an alien came in either side, I'd be an obvious, giant, crusty green monster against a smooth, yellow-lit wall.

I crouched low and peered around the hatch. The room beyond was huge, bigger than the grow-room. Bigger than the factory I'd just walked over. Bigger than one of the transports we'd left behind on the Delta. The same mottled color as the rest of the ship, it was barely illuminated except a wide pool of light far away in the middle of the chamber. Large, dark, indistinct shapes shadowed every corner.

Finally, somewhere to hide.

I slipped around the hatchway and hunkered down behind a long, dark shape.

There was movement in the room and, as my eyes adjusted, flickering blue light. My eyelids were heavy with algae crust, already starting to dry up on my hair and skin.

I pushed up to kneeling and peered over the edge of the long hump I was hiding behind.

The glowing green face of Doc Walsh stared sightlessly back at me.

CHAPTER 8

I scrambled backwards, falling against another of the long mounds, which my eyes finally registered as more of the waist-high woody vines from the factory floor. This huge room was full of them, looping over and under, climbing the walls and hanging from the ceiling. Like the vines in the assembly room, each had a knothole at regular intervals.

But these holes didn't extrude the building plastic.

Some of them were big empty circles, like round lips dotting the edges of the vine.

Some had clear boils erupting from them, with indistinct green shapes inside.

And the one in front of me had a row of unmoving green aliens with Doc Walsh's face.

I was frozen in place, staring at their still, slack features. There was no denying the shape of the nose and the closed, wide-set eyes. They had stubbly, short, green "beards" and long, delicate surgeon's fingers. They appeared to be asleep, and when I tore my eyes from their horrible faces, I saw that their flat feet were plugged into the "lips" on the vine.

All around the room, aliens of all shapes and appendages were plugged into the vines.

With a deep breath, I crawled forward.

Don't do this. You don't want to see.

Every instinct was screaming for me to get out of this dim, unnatural room. But I had to know. A dark, awful suspicion was building in the back of my brain, and I couldn't return to my people until I was certain.

The Doc aliens gave way to another variety with two sets of arms and legs and no head I could recognize. They were so incredibly foreign to my sight that I somehow felt more at ease with them. Truly alien. Nightmare alien. But not alien with a human face.

Nothing in the room moved except me. A blue spark flashed past my knees and I dropped back to the floor, flattening myself against the cool, shadowed surface. The light blinked by again, running the length of the huge wooden vine. What I had taken for a flashlight searching for me was coming from inside the vine itself.

I stood up.

All around the room, the vines were full of chasing blue lights. Branching out among the millions of vines, the lights blinked along at a dizzying speed. It reminded me of a medical teaching video I had watched as part of my early training. The video traced the human nervous system, and messages traveling along the nerves were represented as lights chasing out from the brain, out to the extremities, and back again. The lights rippling along the vines made me feel like I was in a creepy plant version of that video.

So where was the brain?

I peered around the room.

In the middle of the space near the far wall, the lights seemed to converge around a big, dark shadow beneath a cone of light shining on it from above. I couldn't focus on its shape with the disorienting light show all around me, but it looked tubular, wider and taller than a grown man. It gave off no lights of its own, but the longer I watched, the more convinced I became that this was the center of this horrible nightmare.

Dropping to a crawl, I inched forward, trying not to touch any of the vines. But there was no clear passage between them. To move forward, I'd have to climb across them.

Tentatively I reached out with one finger, poking the hard side of one of the vines. It didn't react. No movement, and no light. The top was dotted with the clear boils, and I rose to a crouch, squinting to peer inside the thin bubble wall.

Inside, attached to the vine's hole, was a small green lump. I'd studied embryology enough to recognize an immature life form when I saw one. It had buds for where its arms would form, and a little knob on top that must eventually become a head. Would it have Doc's face? Would it have Maria's?

If I wasn't careful, would it have mine?

Movement at the far wall made me drop back behind the vine. I peered up between the alien boils.

A group of creatures pushed Mr. Albert out from their midst. He stumbled forward and dropped to his knees. They prodded him until he got up, staggering. His hands were tied in front of him, and his ankles tied loosely enough that he could walk. I inched closer and recognized that they had bound his arms with the drawstring from his jacket, and his feet with his own belt.

"Please, don't do this. I'm an engineer. I can help you."
His words rang out in the quiet of the room.

Don't do it. You can't help him. If you do, they'll get you, too.
I was the rest of our people's only hope. I had to find a way
to help them, and at the moment, that meant ignoring the
desperate pleas of one of our own.

They shoved him forward, up some kind of ramp I couldn't
really see behind the huge, tubular structure.

Get closer. You need to see this.

They disappeared up the ramp, and I scrambled over the
vine with the alien buds as quietly as I could. A gap opened
between the vine and the next one, and I scuttled forward as
close as I could get to the bottom of the ramp.

Mr. Albert and the aliens appeared on top. I was close
enough now to see that the big structure was solid at the
bottom, just like the vines that snaked out of its base. As it rose
into the air, its surface changed to the softer, pliable appearance
of the aliens' skin. The vines at its base thrummed with light,
and it pulsed, widening and narrowing. A sickening, slurping
sound was coming from inside it.

The aliens pushed Mr. Albert to the edge of the ramp.

"Please, no. We're humans. We're intelligent creatures.
You can't use us like—"

His voice silenced as they shoved him off the edge. He
plunged into the pulsing tube, disappearing from my sight.

In an instant, the air was filled with screaming. The edge
of the tube pulsed faster, lights flashing all over the room.

It's excited. Whatever it is, it's . . . feeding.

Mr. Albert's screams lasted forever. I slapped my hands
over my ears, flattening my body under the edge of the nearest
vine. It burst with light. The whole room was like some

demented Earth disco, with screaming instead of music and living plant nerves instead of a mirror ball.

Finally, the screaming stopped. The lights faded into a more rhythmic pulsing, and I peeked over the edge. Aliens descended the ramp and fanned out along unoccupied sections of the vine. Those that were carrying guns set them on the ground, and they all plugged themselves into the gaping lips on top of the vines, falling instantly into the catatonic sleep state I'd seen in the Doc Walsh aliens.

I waited, heart hammering, sweat pouring off my face. Every inch of me was still covered in the crusty green slime, and the sweat made it ooze into my eyes. I wiped my face with sticky, green hands, smearing it all into a sticky algae mess.

When the room was silent except for my own hoarse breathing, I peered out again. Everything was still.

Get out of here.

But I had to see.

You're going to die.

But nothing I had seen would help my friends. My brother. The thought of Shane being shoved down into that . . . thing . . . made my stomach heave.

I crawled over more of the vines and inched up the ramp. At the top, I lay down and peeked over the edge.

Below me, bathed in the pool of light from above, a giant mouth opened and closed. Shadows ringed the cavern inside, but I caught bright, rippling flashes in the depths of a liquid bottom. The edges of the mouth were lined with spikes that faced in. Anything that fell or was pushed into that hole would never climb out again.

It belched a great cloud of warm gas. Acid fumes burned my eyes, and I backed away from the edge.

Go now.

I raced down the ramp and bolted through the first open hatchway I found.

CHAPTER 9

I raced away from that awful place, careening down hallways and stumbling through open hatchways. I ran away from any sound I heard with no idea where I was going. The ship was a maze of hallways, and when I finally screeched to a halt in another big open room, my mind came rushing back online.

Hide. Don't get caught.

This room was the familiar glowing blue-green, the smooth walls and floors extruded by the vines. Movement in my peripheral vision sent me scampering behind the first thing large enough to hide me.

It was our shuttle.

I had stumbled into the hangar where our ship had come to rest when the alien vessel swallowed it. I shimmied along the wall behind it, looking for a way in, but the hatch on this side was butted up against the wall of the alien ship. No way to open it.

Our shuttle sat on wheels, and I crawled underneath it. *What are you going to do if you get inside? Even if you could get it out, you don't know how to fly it. And where would you go?* Logically, I knew there was no point, but to the bottom of my soul I craved the familiarity of the smelly interior.

I lay underneath it, peering out from behind one of the wheels.

Aliens were loading crates into the other shuttle.

They were going somewhere.

Anywhere is better than here. Maybe wherever they were going, I could find help. If my headlong flight through this ship had shown me anything, it was that I had no idea at all how to rescue my people from the livestock hold they were prisoners in. And it really was a livestock hold, I realized. For whatever purpose, they were going to be fed one by one into that hideous, toothed mouth-pit.

Get out. Get help.

The aliens shoved a large white crate up a ramp and into the other vessel. It was a long, round craft, made of a metal that looked similar to the hull of our shuttle. Not made out of the smooth, white, extruded material. Another "rescue"? Had it been full of trusting people like us; not humans, but some other species? Had I unknowingly looked into their faces mirrored on some of the aliens' heads? I had no idea how the vine-things worked. How the new aliens were being made to look like us. And if I didn't hurry, no one else would ever know, either.

The green creatures filed out of the other shuttle and through another hatchway.

Now. Go now.

I skittered out from under our shuttle and bolted across the empty floor and up the ramp. Just as I crossed the hatchway, there was noise behind me. The aliens were back, pushing another crate.

Hide.

I was in the cargo area of this ship, surrounded by crates of all sizes. Some were the smooth white I expected. Others were made of metal, and still others of something I didn't recognize. One of the metal crates' lids was slightly ajar. When I heard the aliens' feet on the ramp, I shoved the lid open and jumped inside the crate.

Instantly, I regretted my choice. I landed on a soft surface of something brown and furry. My landing made thick brown dust poof out of whatever the crate was full of, and I choked and gagged on the grit. It filled my nostrils and eyes, and tasted like old mold.

Drool poured out of my mouth, and my nose ran, further gluing the sticky green algae all over my face. When I tried to wipe it, I realized my hands and face were now covered with the brown dust as well, mixed in with the crusty algae. My hair was stiff with it, sticking straight up.

Light disappeared as the aliens slid the lid closed.

I wanted to bang on the top. The air inside was choking, and every move I made released more of the brown dust. But I hunkered down, trying to gag and spit as quietly as I could.

There were tiny slits in the side of the crate, but pressing my eye up to the side just showed me fleeting shadows.

The hold went dark and silent when the aliens closed the hatch. The door locked with a squeal of metal. I wasn't sure if I was alone in the hold. When they attached to the vine, the aliens could go dormant and silent. If I shoved the lid off, would they be sitting all around me? Would they see me? Would they drag me out and throw me into the spiked, acid-filled hole?

I sniffled and drooled, my throat closing around the dust.

A roar of engines split the air, and the whole ship vibrated. In seconds, the hold lost gravity. I floated up against the top, which bumped open. My body drifted out, along with the brown fuzzy surface I'd landed on, which turned out to be some kind of squishy fruit or, possibly, fungus.

There was nothing to grab and nowhere to hide. In the darkness of the hold, I couldn't tell if I was surrounded by aliens. But no one came to push the lid back on, and the base was clearly secured to the floor. Nothing else was floating free. When I finally bumped into the ceiling of the hold, I flailed around, trying to grab onto anything. A thin ridge of pipe provided a grip, and I hauled myself down the side of the ship, grabbing onto the side of another of the metal crates. At some point, we'd land somewhere. I hoped it would be somewhere with gravity, and I'd need to be latched onto the floor so I wouldn't crash down. I hoped it was somewhere with an atmosphere. Oxygen.

The ship hummed and vibrated, presumably flying through space. At some point, I realized I was hungry. The inside of the hold was full of the floating brown furry things, but I had no idea if they were edible or not. I tried licking some of the dried, crusted algae off my hands. It broke apart, and I chewed the coagulated slime, sucking my fingers as clean as I could. But as soon as I used my sticky hands to try and wipe the brown grit from my face, it just smeared into another sticky mess.

The interior brightened, and the ship bucked and shook. I clung to the straps holding the crate down. Gravity grabbed me, and squishy brown blobs rained down. The lid of the metal crate I'd been hiding in crashed to the floor.

My stomach heaved as the shuttle slewed through space.

We're landing.

Soon the hull would be full of aliens, probably unloading all the stuff they'd filled this hull with. Were we going to their home world? If I survived this landing and somehow escaped, would I find myself in a land covered in vines and green creatures?

Won't matter if they find you here.

I clambered back over the edge of the open crate and hunkered down, pulling the brown things still inside over the top of me. If any of me poked out, it would certainly look like the rest of the lumpy stuff. Every inch of me was covered in the sticky brown dust. My throat instantly filled with it again, and I hacked and wheezed, the noise covered by the shrieking of the shuttle's engines.

We bumped down in a hard landing. My forehead smashed into the inside edge of the crate, and everything went black.

CHAPTER 10

When I opened my gritty eyes, I was moving. The crate I was in jostled and jolted. Brown dust still filled my nostrils and throat and I gagged, trying to stay silent. The top had been replaced, and light filtered in through the cracks. When the whole crate tipped diagonally, I realized I'd only been knocked out a few minutes. Aliens were unloading the crate down a ramp.

I didn't have to worry about making noise. Even through the thick metal crate walls, the noise of wherever we were hammered into my head. Metal squealed under the crate as it was hauled onto bumpy ground. Cries of unfamiliar beasts, sharp defined cracks that resulted in more wordless screaming, and yelling voices in no language I had ever heard echoed in the little box.

At least there was air. I tried to take a deeper breath but had to choke back another round of gagging coughs.

One of the cracks in the side of the crate was a bit larger than the rest. I eased myself over to it, trying not to jostle the moving box and alert the aliens to my presence, and pushed my face up against the edge. Images flitted by the tiny slit.

Huge, lumbering beasts, too large for me to see their length through the crack.

Scores of other boxes.

Hurrying shadows of all shapes against a dull gray sky.

And right next to me, one of the green alien creatures I'd come to loathe and fear.

The sky darkened, and the crate stopped moving. Through the little slit, I could see the aliens move away, and a relative quiet descended in the box. I thought from the echoes that I was probably in some kind of shelter, maybe a warehouse. There were noises all around, but nothing right up next to my crate.

No decent slits to see out of on the other side—I'd have to chance it.

Fast or slow? Fling off the top and run for it, or try for stealth?

Like a descendant of some tiny mammal that hid in the shadows of dinosaurs so many millions of years ago on the long-gone planet Earth, I opted for stealth. Pushing up with my shoulder against the top of the crate, I braced my legs against the sides. It slowly slid away to reveal a draped gray cloth far overhead. I was in some kind of tent.

Just a little farther and I'd be able to get out.

The crate lid overbalanced and crashed to the floor with a huge clatter.

Voices shouted. I couldn't understand the words, but the tone was unmistakable.

I leaped from the crate and bolted away.

HORIZON DELTA

My eyes took in the scene of chaos around me as I wove through heaps of stacked crates, barrels, and piled-up foods. A thick rope cordoned off what must be my familiar aliens' merchandise area from the rest, and I tried to vault over it, but my foot caught and I tumbled down.

The voices were closer, shouting and squeaking. None of them sounded human.

I scrambled to my feet and pushed off. Shapes closed in around me, large, lumpy things I didn't dare stop to stare at. They were bigger than I was, and slower. I ducked away, sliding under the curtained edge of the tent, and came up squinting into the brighter gray light.

As I ran, my mind started to process the sights that streamed by. Other huge tent-buildings off to either side. Makeshift stalls of what looked like wood closer in. Dirt under my feet.

And aliens. Everywhere I turned, aliens.

How could there be so many? I raced down the crowded street, knocking creatures out of my way. Hairy legs and smooth tentacles, tiny squeaking things underfoot and great lumbering beasts that shadowed the gray light.

Run. Hide.

With no idea where safety might be, much less help, I careened on. The shouts behind me turned to shouts ahead, and the crowd around me parted. Thick hands grabbed me from behind and spun me around by the shoulders.

I looked up into a face. It had eyes and open-holed nostrils in roughly the right places. The mouth was a lipless slit full of large, square teeth. Short, bristly hairs poked out of every surface, and the huge sloping shoulders reminded me of gorillas from the Delta's nature videos.

Three similar faces crowded around me, and more hands grabbed me. Each hand had only four fingers, but each was as thick as my wrist.

The first face barked at me. It waited a moment, then barked again.

It's trying to talk to you. Tell it. Ask it for help.

I opened my mouth to answer, but all that came out was a gurgling hack. My throat and nostrils were still raw from the brown dust. I looked down at my arms to see I was still caked head to toe in the green algae slime swirled with brown filth.

They've never seen a human before, and even if they have, you don't look human, my logical mind offered, but my panicked brain screamed, drowning it out.

I tried again to speak but just gagged out a gob of brown goo.

The huge things barked to each other. One of them picked me up and slung me over its shoulder. I beat at it with grimy fists and feet, but it was like beating a wall. The crowds parted to let us through and re-formed behind the beast. Alien faces glanced up at me, then turned back to their own.

The beast carried me through what must have been a marketplace, out to the edge of the tents and stalls. In the distance sat shuttle after shuttle, parked around an open piece of ground. I thought I recognized the one I had ridden down on right in the middle. Was it that one with the round nose? Or was it the other one on the left?

My mind was nearly shut down with panic, and this was the last straw.

You don't know which shuttle. How are you going to get back to Shane?

I slumped over the creature's back.

HORIZON DELTA

It didn't matter where it was taking me. Didn't matter what it planned to do with me. I'd lost the green aliens' shuttle, and I'd never find my way back to the invisible black ship that must be orbiting somewhere far overhead with what remained of the human race inside.

I had risked everything to escape captivity and save them.
I had failed.

CHAPTER 11

The beast carried me into a wooden stockade with thick walls and metal mesh over the top. It threw me down, knocking the wind out of me, and retreated through a heavy gate that squealed shut. As soon as I could breathe, I rolled over onto my hands and knees and hacked and wheezed, coughing up thick blobs of brown dust phlegm. My throat was raw, and my eyes still full of grit. The dirt of this place was settling on my skin, mixing with the flaking green and brown.

I must look like an alien myself.

And I guess I am.

This wasn't the Delta. It wasn't Earth. It wasn't far-off Chara d, where we had dreamed of our descendants landing in another hundred years.

It was just . . . somewhere. And to whoever lived here, I was the alien.

I became aware that I wasn't alone in the stockade.

Small, slimy creatures slithered around my ankles. There were a dozen of them in here, skittering around the dirt ground, climbing up the walls, and hanging from the mesh overhead. Each one had a hundred tiny legs and was as long and thick as my thigh. They were all varying shades of orange with brown heads. At least, I assumed they were heads. When they slithered and climbed, the brown end went first. They appeared to be climbing out a tiny hole in a large crate near my cage.

There was a small group of four-legged creatures huddled on one side of the fenced-in pen. Long necks held narrow heads with small, pinched muzzles. Thick, shaggy white hair covered them from the eyes down, and they pushed against each other, clearly trying to hide behind each other. They climbed up the sides of the mesh as high as they could before dropping down, screaming shrill, grating cries.

Hide with them.

But when I approached, they scattered, bolting around me, their huge feet crushing some of the orange slitherers on the ground. They re-formed their huddle on the other side. I stood alone in the middle of the pen.

Outside, a smaller crowd flowed by.

No creature got too close to the mesh fencing with the loose orange things dangling off it. My pulse throbbed in my skull as they all gave the pen a wide berth, pointing with clawed hands or blunt appendages but not approaching.

I bet these orange things are venomous.

One of them slithered across my foot, and I jumped back, squishing another under my heel.

"Help!" The word came out in a scratchy, grating squawk. "Help! Get me out of here! Those things are getting out!"

The noise of my cries blended in with the cacophony all around me. Other pens surrounded the one I was in, holding other creatures I couldn't identify. None of the rest had wire mesh over the top. But it didn't look like any of the other beasts could climb.

"Someone! Anyone!" My voice was starting to come back. I could almost understand myself. But no one stopped.

I kept yelling, standing stock-still in the middle of the pen, afraid to move too close to the walls where the orange things dangled overhead. *I bet they bite.*

The gate opened and one of the gorilla-beasts lumbered in. It carried a large bag with a long, thin neck, and a long stick with pincers on the end, and it wore tall, thick boots and a heavy cloak. *Yeah, the orange things are venomous.* The white shaggy things bolted away from it, and I danced aside to avoid getting trampled. I raced for the gate, but another gorilla-beast closed it.

The first one reached out with the pincers and grabbed one of the orange things, sticking the pincer down through the neck of the bag and pulling it out empty. The bag wriggled in the beast's grasp as it grabbed another of the orange things and stuffed it in.

"Help me! You have to help me!"

The gorilla-beast looked up at my shout, then dropped its eyes back to the ground and grabbed another orange thing. It didn't even seem surprised that they were escaping through a hole in their crate.

Gotta get out of here.

I shuffled forward, kicking away the slithering, hundred-leggers. "Please, you have to get me out of here."

When I had almost reached the gorilla-beast, it grabbed another orange thing and thrust the pincer with the wriggling thing straight at me. I jerked to a halt, the horrible brown head inches from my face. It whipped on the end of the stick, its hundred little legs writhing at me.

The gorilla eyed me for a moment, stuffed the orange thing into the bag, and turned back for the gate. I rushed up behind it, and without looking, it swung a fist out and shoved me back away from the gate. Its friend opened the gate, and the beast slipped through, slamming it shut right in my face.

The whole structure rattled, and something plopped right onto my head. I screamed and flung my hands up, scratching at the fat orange bug crawling in my hair, sending it flying into the wall.

A gargling scream tore from my throat, and I felt the crust on my face crack. My hair was stiff and standing up as I frantically beat at my head, certain I could still feel the thing slithering around my ears.

Outside the mesh, the gorilla dumped the contents of the bag into a large box. A tall, thin creature with a pointed head and two huge, yellow eyes handed over a few bright silver stones and took the box from the gorilla.

It just bought those creatures. This is a market, and they're for sale.

I looked out into the crowds passing between the fenced-in pens.

All these things were for sale.

And so am I.

CHAPTER 12

I crept as close to the mesh as I dared.

"Please save me. Please help me." My voice was still a raw, scratchy mess, but no one evidenced any recognition that I was speaking words. *They must think I'm just some other dumb beast, bleating against the walls of its cage.*

None of the aliens that passed were any version of the green ones that held my people captive. And what would I do if one of them passed? Was I better off with them? At least if they found me, they'd take me back to my brother. I could die with other humans instead of here, on this foreign world, surrounded by alien livestock.

Long hours passed.

The gorillas would come into the cage and grab a bagful of the orange bugs or herd out a couple of the white shaggy things, always forcing me away from the gate. More of the silver stones changed hands. My already devastated throat grew more raw as the day passed without water, and a dusty wind blew more grit into my face. My pleas for help got weaker, and finally I gave up, sinking down onto the dry ground. Orange bugs slithered near me, and I ignored them. It didn't matter. Wherever and however I died, surely it would be over soon. In all my panic, I hadn't realized how chilly it was here. I shivered, curling into a ball on the ground.

Four tall figures passed the mesh. Their shadows passed over me, and I glanced up. All of them wore long, black, hooded cloaks. Sharp beaks poked out the fronts, with wicked, downward-curving hooks on the ends. Taloned hands poked out the sleeves.

I didn't even bother to whisper for help. No one on this planet could possibly understand me.

The figures glided past. I wiped more brown snot from my nose, scraping my hands against my red, swollen eyes. All of the panic of the day had drained out of me, leaving me empty and exhausted. Despair clouded my vision, and my dry mouth tasted like ashy death.

One of the figures stopped and stared in at me. The hood shadowed its face, but the beak poking out reminded me of a falcon's, or maybe an eagle's. Its hands were buried in the folds of the cloak, which dragged the ground. Another of its kind returned to join it, and they made strange whistling noises to each other. Both of them were staring right at me.

Oh, no.

They're going to buy me.

And they're going to eat me.

I had no doubt of it. These were predators. The second one's talons were as long as my little finger, and its feet were wrinkled skin with talons on the end. It pointed in at me, and one of the gorillas pointed its stick at me. The hooded thing pulled out a few of the shiny stones, and the gorilla snorted, clearly a negative.

They bargained. The gorilla gestured and barked, and the taloned thing flapped its arms, the cloak billowing out. Inside was a flash of iridescent green.

I looked down at my own green-plastered skin. *It probably thinks I look delicious.*

The gorilla barked again. *That's right*, I silently willed it. *Don't sell me to those monsters. Just let me stay here. Or anywhere.*

More of the silver stone glinted in the yellow, taloned hand.

No. Please, no. I jumped to my feet and waved my arms, trying to look less like food. "Go away!" I shouted. "I'm not your dinner."

The first figure spun to stare at me. It made a gesture, raising one finger of a gloved hand to its beak. The gesture stopped me cold. If the thing had made a noise, I would have sworn it would have been to shush me.

Stunned, I stopped flapping around.

The gorilla took the stones, and the gate swung open. I stood there, shoulders slumped and head hanging as the beast lumbered in and picked me up. Like a sack of potatoes, I hung over its back. It plopped me down in front of one of the tall, hooded figures, and I looked up into the hood.

I was right. It was an eagle.

Sharp, black eyes peered down at me from a pale-green feathered face. It clacked its beak and whistled, a high, chirping noise that must have been its language. When it reached for me with its talons, I got a glimpse of the body covered in darker green feathers tipped with golden yellow. The thing that was going to eat me was beautiful. At least there was that.

71

Talons grabbed my left shoulder, and the other figure grabbed my right. Its talons were much shorter, covered in black gloves, and it didn't speak. The feathers around its glassy eyes were light brown with black edges.

I didn't even fight as they guided me away from the livestock pens. The other two walked behind us, and the strength of the talons digging into my shoulder told me there was no escape. I shuffled along between them.

They whistled and chirped back and forth. It was getting dark, and most of the stalls were empty. They pulled me into one and lowered a thick, brown curtain over the front. One of them pulled from its cloak a small silver disk. It tapped the disk with a talon, and it lit up with bright white light. I squinted and turned my face away.

The gloved one spun me around, gripping my shoulders on each side. I peered up into its brown face, and it cocked its head, turning this way and that. It wiped my face with a glove and pulled at the crust in my hair.

"Cut it out," I muttered. "Just eat me already."

The bird-thing stopped and gazed at me for a moment. Its shoulders jumped in what looked like laughter. The other three chirped and peered at me.

"Eat you?" The words were clear, unaccented English, and my heart nearly stopped. "There are a lot of words I could use to describe you right now, kid, but 'food' isn't one of them. Although I swear that's a carrot stuck in your hair."

I raised a hand and pulled at the spot it was touching, pulling out a dried-up chunk of alien algae-carrot.

The thing raised its gloved hand and grabbed its own beak. It pulled, and the whole thing came off, beak and feathers together. *A mask. A bird mask.*

It lowered its hood. The face that looked at me was as human as mine, with clear olive skin and heavy brown eyes. Long black hair streaked with gray was tied back in a knot. It pulled off the glove, revealing strong, calloused hands.

The man leaned down and smiled at me.

"I don't know who you are, kid, or how in the stars you got here." The grin crinkled his eyes and my mouth dropped open as he continued. "But my name is Shiro Yamoto, and this is your lucky day."

CHAPTER 13

A million questions flooded my exhausted brain, but before I could get any of them out, one of the birdpeople jerked its head to the side and gave a cautious whistle. The human who called himself Shiro raised a finger to his lips again and pulled me close, hunkering down to my height. The five of us stood frozen as heavy footsteps passed the front of the curtained-off stall.

When the sounds had passed and we all started to breathe again, I took a good look at the other birdmens' faces. All of them had moving eyelids that blinked, and their nostrils flared when they breathed. Only Shiro was a human in a bird mask. The rest were real birdpeople.

"We need to get you out of here," Shiro said. "And nobody needs to know what a human looks like." His face split into a grin. "Darned lucky you're all mucked up with green stuff. I don't think anybody here would recognize what you really look like underneath all that slime and dirt."

I patted my crunchy hair, which was standing straight out at all angles from my head. *Yeah, that's a carrot in there.*

"But where—" I began, and Shiro cut me off.

"Time for all your questions later. And time for all of mine." He nodded to the birdmen. "Let's get you back to our ship so they can finish their transaction and get us out of here. Not the safest place to be after dark."

I shook out of his grasp. "Look, thanks for rescuing me and all, but I can't go with you. My brother and the rest of my people are captives on a ship in orbit. I came down here on a shuttle, and I'm not going anywhere until I find that shuttle. I need to get back to my brother."

Shiro's eyes narrowed. "What shuttle? How many people? Where did you . . ." He shook his head. "Nope. No time now." He whistled to the birdmen, and one of them peered out the front of the stall for a moment before whistling back. Shiro turned around and pulled out a knife, cutting down a large swath of the thick brown curtain hanging from the back of the stall. He whipped it around my head and shoulders, creating a makeshift cloak for me. "Look, we can sort it all out once we're somewhere safer. Keep this over your head, and don't look at anyone. Stay close to me and we'll get to our ship. Then we can figure out where your people are and what to do about them."

I started to protest, but he fixed my gaze in a stern glare. I shut up and nodded.

Finally. Someone who can be in charge of all this. As much as I wanted to race from the stall and find the green aliens' ship, the weariness of the day had caught up to me. Shiro was a human. He would help me sort this out. I finally had allies who could help me rescue my brother.

Shiro replaced his bird mask and pulled up the hood, shadowing his face. It was a good mask. Under that hood, no one would guess he was anything other than a real birdman. We shuffled out of the stall, and I stayed pressed up against Shiro's side. The sun had nearly set and the area around the livestock pens was almost deserted. Shiro placed a gloved hand on my shoulder, and I moved in closer to his cloaked side. I didn't dare look up to see where we were going, but soon we had left the pens full of bleating, snarling, and wailing animals behind us and moved out into the long shadows of the parked shuttles. After a long walk, he squeezed my shoulder, and I looked up to see a huge, sleek, silver craft in front of us. It was narrow at the front, with wide, triangular wings at the back. A hatchway opened with a hiss, and a long ramp descended. We trooped up the ramp, and Shiro guided me through a large cargo bay and through another small hatch into the cockpit area. It had two rows of seats behind what must be the pilot's chair and dark windows down each side.

"Sit here and be quiet," he said, striding forward into the control area. "We're here to do some trading, and then we'll be on our way. We'll figure out who has our people and what to do once we're off this world."

Our people? I pressed my face up against the window. Shiro reached out and flipped a switch, one of a thousand controls labeled in a scratchy language that looked like no writing I'd ever seen. Outside the shuttle, the ground lit up around us.

"Stay here and stay silent," he said. "You can take the curtain off your head now, but I'm locking the door behind me. We'll be back and we'll get out of here." He slipped out the hatch behind me, and I heard a click after it closed.

The very end of the ramp was in view if I craned my neck backwards. The other three birdmen glided down to the bottom of the ramp and stood waiting. Shiro, his mask replaced and hood pulled up, joined them. In a moment, dark shadows plodded around the side of the shuttle next to us, a big, black, hulking thing shaped like a pyramid.

When the shadows moved into the light, my heart skipped a beat.

"It's them!" My voice echoed in the empty cockpit. "Oh, stars, it's them!"

Nine of the familiar green aliens clustered around the birdmen at the bottom of the ramp. Even at this distance, I was certain one of them was Eddie. I jumped up and turned to the hatch, but it didn't open despite my pounding. When I scuttled back to my seat and peered out the window again, Shiro's mask was staring straight at me. I could feel his glare through the glass eyes and shrank into my seat under its force.

As soon as they open this hatch, I'm out of here. Gotta follow them. Find my brother.

The green aliens produced five small boxes, setting them on the ground in front of them and stepping back. The birdmen picked them up and opened them in turns, peering in and appearing to sniff the contents. They whistled to each other and set the boxes on the ground again.

Shiro and two of the birdmen disappeared up the ramp. Soon they reappeared with two large crates and a sealed tub. The green aliens peered into the crates and lifted the lid on the tub, checking out the contents. Apparently satisfied, one of the greens produced a small chip and handed it to one of the birdmen. The birdman handed back a similar chip. Was it payment or a receipt?

The aliens dragged the crates and tub away, and Shiro and the birdmen carried the small boxes they had traded for up the ramp. Through the back wall of the cockpit, I heard the ramp retract and the large hatchway slam shut. As soon as the small hatch opened, I jumped at Shiro.

"That's the ones! That's who has my brother!"

He pulled off the mask and stared at me. "Are you certain? They all look different. Are you sure those are the ones?"

I nodded, trying to shove my way past him, but the others blocked my way. "It's them. We have to make them give our people back!"

Shiro's face fell. "I hope you're wrong, kid. I really hope you're wrong." He glanced out the window to where the green aliens had disappeared, heading back to wherever their shuttle waited. "Because if the Botanists have your people, then wherever you came from, you're the only survivor."

CHAPTER 14

Ignoring my pleas to follow the green aliens, Shiro shoved me back into my seat. "Buckle up, kid. It's going to be a rough takeoff."

One of the birdmen climbed into the seat in the front with the most controls, and Shiro sat next to him. The other two pulled off their cloaks and sat in the seats opposite me, peering at me and whistling softly. In addition to the iridescent green one I had seen, these other two were varying shades of brown, with soft, shiny eyes and golden beaks. As panicked as I was about finding my brother, I couldn't help but wonder at the soft feathers that covered them from face to foot.

One held out a taloned hand, and I tentatively reached out. It didn't make any threatening move and clearly wanted me to touch it. I pulled one of my fingers over the back of the wrinkled hand and tapped a nail against the long, black talon. The birdman chirped and did the same to me, running a talon gently down the back of my crusty green hand.

Birdpeople. I thought about the science I had learned aboard Horizon Delta, back in the days when we thought education would matter. If these birdpeople were anything like the birds of long-dead Earth, these brown-shaded ones were probably females, and the yellow-green one was a male. Time I stopped thinking of them as "it." I had never made a distinction like that with the green aliens that held me captive.

The roar of the engines made conversation impossible, and the birdwomen settled back, pulling safety harnesses over their shoulders. I reached back and found a similar harness, and one of the birdwomen helped me fasten it. I was much smaller than they were, and it hung loose around me, so I gripped the armrest, so similar to the ones on the Delta shuttles.

The ship lifted off the ground with a lurch and hurtled into the sky. I peered out the window as the alien marketplace, dimly lit below me, grew more distant. Soon the sky around us was full of stars, and I relaxed a bit. I was used to a sky full of stars.

Soon we began to grow lighter in our seats as the ship escaped the nameless planet's gravity.

With a clunk, gravity suddenly reasserted itself, and I bounced back down in the harness. One of the birdwomen looked over, a concerned look in her eyes. I tried to smile at her, dry lips cracking at the edges. Artificial gravity in a shuttle? Well, why not? The green creatures had used some kind of gravity in their huge black bean. Whatever the technology, it must work on this smaller scale as well.

I turned back to the window, searching in vain for a black hole in the stars that might indicate where the ship holding my brother was hiding. But the glitter all around was unbroken. If the black bean ship was out there, it wasn't where I was looking.

The engine noise changed, and I leaned into the aisle to look out the front of the shuttle. Something huge and silver was out there, with a big, gaping black hatch. As I watched, we slowed and the engines cut off. Our shuttle glided through the hatch and into a huge open bay. Gravity pulled harder on me as soon as the shuttle nosed inside, and the front tipped downward, coming to rest on the floor of the hatch. Lights outside the window clicked brighter, and a creaking, grinding noise squealed around us. In a moment, the creaking stopped, and my ears popped with a change in pressure. A deep, rumbling hum thrummed through my feet. We were inside a much larger ship.

The birdwomen unhooked their harnesses and stood up. I followed them out the now-unlocked hatch behind us, and Shiro followed me. The iridescent green pilot stayed in his seat, clicking his talons on the shuttle's controls.

I opened my mouth to start asking questions, but Shiro shook his head. "Come on, kid. Let's get you cleaned up and fed. Then we'll sit down and figure all this out together." I was too tired to argue.

We trooped down the ramp into the hangar. Uncloaked birdpeople scuttled around us, securing our shuttle to the floor of the hangar. They stopped and stared when they saw me, but a few reassuring whistles from Shiro seemed to relax them.

"What are you saying?" I asked him.

He smiled. "Just told them you were a human, like me."

"They know about humans?" I felt silly as soon as the words slipped out. Of course they did. They had Shiro, didn't they?

My brain finally started making sense of things.

"Are you from the Alpha or the Beta?"

He snorted. "I'm Alpha. And you must be Delta?"

I nodded. "What's left of us."

His eyes lost their twinkle and grew somber. "Yeah, aren't we all? What's left of us, for sure."

He led me through a doorway and down a long, clean hallway into an elevator. We passed birdpeople of every color—from sapphire blues to silvery whites. They all whistled questions to Shiro, who whistled back.

"You can understand them?" I asked once the elevator doors closed and it was just the two of us.

"I've been with this ship for almost twenty years now, kid." He chuckled for a moment. "Kid. What's your actual name?"

"Jonah Campbell."

He removed the black gloves and held out a hand. I shook it, formally.

"Nice to meet you, Jonah," he said, stuffing the gloves into his pants pocket. The clothes he wore were cut like a Horizon uniform but made from some kind of softer material in a dark brown color. His boots were the nicest I'd ever seen.

My eyes were heavy as the elevator stopped and we stepped out into a wide hall. Rows of tables filled the room, and birdpeople dotted them. A bright, clean smell made my stomach growl, though I'd never smelled anything like it.

Shiro guided me away from the large room and down another hallway. "First things first," he said. "This can be your room." He waved a hand at a panel outside a doorway, which slid open without a sound. Inside was a small room with a pile of blankets folded on a low cot. Shiro pushed me toward a smaller room off the main one. In there I found a round hatch on the floor that opened when Shiro waved at a panel over it.

"Toilet," he said unnecessarily. There was a bowl under a tap, obviously a sink, and a large, empty tub. "This is a human room, made for human crew. Birdpeople all sleep in groups. Flocks, really. They aren't much for showers," he said with a smile, "but they do love a bath." He showed me how to work the controls, sending steaming water into the tub. "Get yourself washed up. I'll set some clean clothes out in your room. Then we can get some food and you can tell me how under all the stars a human from Horizon Delta ended up in a livestock pen on Reganus Five."

CHAPTER 15

The bath was heaven. I had to drain and refill it three times before the water dripping off me was anything but green and slimy. There wasn't anything I recognized as soap, so I just used my hands to scrub at my skin and hair until I thought I probably looked human again. The hot water made me even drowsier.

Gotta stay awake. Gotta make a plan.

A knock on the wall of the bathroom made me jump. I realized I had fallen asleep in the tub, water cooling around me.

Shiro held out a towel. "Here you go. Dry off and get dressed. I'll meet you in the hall."

I wiped myself dry, still finding bits of green that stained the beige towel. All the clothes were too big on me. Probably his own. I hadn't seen any other humans on the ship and assumed he was the only one. The shirt hung on me, but there was a belt to hold up the pants. I rolled up the cuffs and pulled on socks. My own shoes were probably beyond saving, unless the bird ship had some kind of miraculous laundry service. *Why not? They have gravity.* And whatever smelled so good in that big dining hall. There was a pair of boots like Shiro's on the floor, and they almost fit. I tightened the straps that held them around my ankles and exited the little room.

Shiro met me in the corridor, and I followed him back to the tables. Three other humans and two birdmen were waiting at a table. All three of the humans looked about twenty, two guys and a girl. The birdmen were the browns and creams I assumed were female.

Shiro handed me a small, silver cuff. It looked like a tiny bracelet, and I held it in my fingers.

"Put it on," one of the guys said, pulling back his hair to show me how his ear held a similar cuff. "It's a translator."

I slipped the cuff on my ear and winced at a high-pitched squeal. The noise subsided, and suddenly the whistling of all the birdpeople around the room turned into the murmur of conversation. My eyes widened.

"Those things took forever to program."

I whipped my head from face to face, finally realizing it was one of the birdwomen that had spoken. Around the English translation, I had heard her normal whistling language, but the words spoken into my ear from the translator cuff were quiet and clear.

"Pretty neat, huh?" That was Shiro. The cuff didn't translate that, and I realized it would take my brain a while to sort out listening to the combination of real words spoken at normal volume, and whistles turned into English in my ear. It was hard to tell who was speaking at the moment.

"You don't wear one?" I hadn't noticed Shiro sporting a similar cuff back on the planet.

"Nope. I speak Siitsi pretty well."

One of the females made a little titter that had to be a laugh. It wasn't words, because my cuff didn't translate it.

Shiro made a face at her. "I said pretty well. Not perfect." He turned to the rest of the table. "Everybody, this is Jonah."

I nodded at my name.

He introduced the two human guys as Ricky and Corey. The girl was Priya.

"And this is . . ." He made two distinct whistles, indicating the two birdwomen. Again, no translation in my ear. "Until you can make their Siitsi names, call them Weetzy and Tishi."

The names sounded odd to me. "Siitsi names?"

The human girl, Priya, nodded. "Siitsi is what they are. Birdpeople, to us. It's the closest translation to the whistle they use."

I noticed that the two Siitsi females sported cuffs like ours on tiny ears I hadn't realized they had under their feathers. "Their cuffs translate English into . . . Siitsi?"

The lighter cream-colored one named Tishi whistled, and my cuff translated. "Yes. We understand a lot of your language, but you talk so fast when you're together." It was still disorienting to hear her whistling but also get the words straight into my ears. She continued, "We can't make the sounds you make, but some of you can learn to make our words." She turned an eye to Shiro.

I shook my head. "Okay, this is . . . well, it's frankly astounding. And I'm sure once I have a minute to think about it, I'll be properly amazed at all this." I indicated everything—

the ship around me, the birdpeople, the humans. "But right now, we need to figure out how to get my people back."

The others leaned in as I told my story. How the Delta broke down year after year, leaving us adrift. How the huge black bean swallowed our shuttle. How they took us captive and I escaped in the vat of algae. Shiro's lips curled up at that.

"I remember that stuff." He sniffed. "Grew up on it a million years ago on the Alpha."

Another birdperson, a bright yellow male, arrived with trays of multicolored, soft-looking squares. I inhaled as a plate was set in front of me. This was the scent I'd noticed on the way through. Everyone around me was picking up the squares and shoving them into their mouths.

I tasted one. Sweet, soft, full of juice. I closed my eyes and sighed.

"First time eating fresh fruit?" Shiro asked.

There weren't words, even if my mouth weren't stuffed full. I just nodded and shoved in another bite.

"Not so fast," he cautioned. "There's plenty of it. Don't want to get sick."

But I didn't care. We had grown some vegetables in the gardens on the Delta, at least until the power shut off. I knew what carrots tasted like, and beets, and parsnips. But I'd only seen fruit trees in videos and read about them in books. The reality was so much sweeter.

Conversation paused for a moment as I filled my aching stomach.

"So tell me again about the ship," Shiro said. "It swallowed your shuttle?"

I described what I remembered. "It was like it just . . . yeah, swallowed us. And ate through the edges of the

Delta so we didn't lose our hatch pressure. And then we were inside it."

"Wait," Priya said. "The ship was invisible against the sky?" She exchanged a look with Corey. "You don't think . . ."

He shook his head with a glance at me.

My story continued with the sounds of other creatures behind other hatchways. The factory floor where the plastic-looking stuff was being made into all kinds of things. The guns. The huge, woody vines and the aliens that all looked different, plugged into tiny mouths on the vines.

"Botanists," Corey said. His light eyes narrowed to slits. "We call them Botanists. It's who we went to Reganus Five to trade with. They can make anything you want, and all they want to be paid in is organics . . . animals, seeds, eggs, other plants."

I raised an eyebrow. "Other plants?"

Priya nodded. "They're plants, of course. We've known that since they started showing up on trade worlds. The little ones they send down to do the trading don't talk. Always little and green, but different shapes. They seem . . . almost like little robots. They must have some kind of rudimentary brains, but they don't ever seem to think on their own, and if you don't do exactly what they expect you to do, they just skitter away."

Corey was tapping a thumbnail thoughtfully against his teeth. "We've always thought they were a hive mind of some kind . . . programmed by something more intelligent on their home world or on a mother ship. No way were those little things capable of space travel on their own."

I thought about the huge room full of vines that lit up like nerves all around.

"I think you're right," I said. "I think there's one giant brain running the whole ship. They have these vines that they plug into and just seem to . . . go to sleep." I felt like an idiot for not realizing it sooner. Of course they were buds off the larger plant. The giant pitcher in the center that ate Mr. Albert.

And Doc Walsh.

It was the center of the brain that controlled all the little green plant aliens.

"Is it possible they're using all the things they trade for to . . . program new ones?" I told them about Doc Walsh. How he'd been taken away and, a few days later, new Botanists were budding that had his face.

Ricky's eyes lit up. "DNA. Of course they are!" He turned to Priya. "It's why they only want organics. Somehow they're reading the new DNA and using it to differentiate into new forms."

I shook my head. "Not reading it. It eats them." They stared at me as I told them about the huge pitcher in the middle of the nerve nest. I left out all the screaming when they threw in Mr. Albert.

"It's the mouth and the brain," Priya said. "It must dissolve things down to proteins and use that to evolve itself. All the Botanists we've ever seen must be part of one huge organism." She exchanged another worried look with Corey but said nothing more.

All the science was making my head spin. My eyelids were getting heavy, my head nodding in exhaustion.

"Okay, I think we've got enough to ponder for tonight," Shiro said. "Let's get Jonah some sleep, and tomorrow we'll figure out where we go from here."

We all stood up from the table, and I stumbled back to my room.

Shiro stood outside my open doorway. "If you need anything, just touch this panel and say what you need." He showed me a panel on the inside of the doorway. "It understands English."

"But what about my brother? My people?" I could barely form the sentence.

He gave me a gentle push toward the pile of blankets. "Tonight, you need to sleep. Tomorrow we'll figure out how to rescue your brother."

I turned to watch the doorway slide closed. He tried to hide it behind an encouraging smile, but even as tired as I was, I could tell he was lying.

Shiro didn't believe I would ever see my brother again.

CHAPTER 16

I slept like the dead. Some number of hours later, a high-pitched beeping woke me. It didn't stop until I yelled, "Shut up!" and I realized it was coming from the panel by the door. In a few minutes, Shiro's voice piped through the panel.

"Jonah, you awake? I'll send somebody to get you in a couple of minutes."

I grumbled a response and shoved the blankets off me. The room was dim, and I sat up from the cot. I grumbled some more, swinging my legs unsteadily to the floor.

Bathroom time. The sink water flowed warm, and as much as I longed to get into the bathtub again, I figured Shiro would want me soon. The clothes he had given me were the only ones I had, and they were rumpled from sleep. I hitched the belt up on the pants, put on the boots, and waved a hand in front of the panel. The door slid open, and a bright blue birdman waited outside. *Siitsi,* I reminded myself. *They aren't really birds.*

I examined him more closely as he led me through the corridors of the ship. He walked upright, but his legs didn't bend like mine. I remembered from anatomy classes I'd taken in preparation for my doctor's training that many Earth animals had similar anatomy, just put together in different proportions. What I thought of as knees were probably the Siitsi's ankles, which is why they looked like they hinged in the wrong direction. The blue Siitsi hadn't spoken to me, and if there was a translator cuff in the feathers on his head, I couldn't see it.

The ship was a confusing maze. At times we passed open doors that all seemed to be labs of some type or another. No one looked up from whatever they were working on as we passed. But most of the doors were closed, just long hallways of silver hatchways.

We rode the elevator—a different one from last night, at least I thought so—down. There weren't any buttons on the panel, which confused me until the Siitsi whistled to it. No lights illuminated to show us how many floors we descended. It could have been three very slowly, or thirty very fast. Once off the elevator, he led me to another closed door that opened to his wave.

"Jonah! Come in. We were just talking about you."

Shiro sat at a long table, along with Priya and the cream-colored Siitsi from last night, Tishi. Corey stood with his back to us, studying a holographic image that seemed to be emitting from a panel on the counter in front of him. The lettering was more of the scratchy language I now assumed was the written form of Siitsi. The image looked like blueprints, hastily drawn with a lot of scratching out, things circled, and arrows pointing at other things. Totally incomprehensible to me.

The back wall of the room held several large aquariums of clear water. Inside, hideous, fist-sized pale crustacean-type creatures crawled around under large, black rocks.

Shiro pushed a covered bowl across the table and motioned for me to sit down. "I brought you breakfast."

There was more fruit in the bowl, along with some kind of warm, soft grain. I inhaled it, pouring the last bits right into my mouth from the bowl.

"So we've been thinking about the ship you described," Priya said, "and we think we know how they do it."

"Do what?" I wiped my chin on my sleeve.

"How the ship is invisible like that," she said.

Corey spoke up, gesturing at the hologram. "We know the Botanists are plants. Or maybe just one plant, with a whole bunch of independent buds. And now, thanks to you, we know they probably use DNA from all the alien life forms they trade for on the trade worlds to allow them to make whatever they want. They're extruding the materials they make stuff out of, and we think their whole ship might be part of the same giant organism."

Priya nodded. "We think the ship itself might be alive in a way. Connected to the 'brain' you saw, which is how it managed to open up and swallow your shuttle." She gestured to the holographic blueprints. "Plants can absorb all different wavelengths of light, which they use for photosynthesis to make their own energy. And if the outside of their ship is made of plant material, they could have it absorb whatever wavelengths they need. Whatever isn't absorbed is reflected back as color, so if it absorbs all visible light, it's black. Totally invisible. Impossible to track."

"And it's not like no one has tried," Shiro said, brow furrowing. "They always show up in a regular metal shuttle to a trade world. Probably something they scavenged, or maybe even hijacked from space. The things they make that we trade for . . . they're incredibly valuable, and no one knows how they do it. You tell them what you need, and sometime later, you go pick it up. They make new things out of nothing."

I frowned. "Not out of nothing. Out of people and animals they feed to the pitcher."

"Right." Priya tried to look sad about that, but she was obviously too excited about the science. "So here's the thing. We trade with the Botanists because they make things no one else can. And every time someone has tried to follow them back to their home world to see how they do it, the shuttle they're following just disappears."

"The black bean ship swallows them up, and away they go." My face felt hot at the mention. *It swallowed us, too.*

"Right," Priya said again. "They're scavengers, and sometimes sell things they've obviously taken from other ships."

Shiro's face darkened. "They're invaders and criminals."

I shuddered. They really were criminals. "Do they steal things? Take the people if they land somewhere else?"

"Worse." The voice came through my ear cuff, and I watched Tishi's face as she spoke. Her stiff beak showed no expression, but she made up for it with her huge brown eyes. "We weren't sure until you told us about the vines. We suspected it might be the same species, but no one ever survived an invasion, so nobody was certain. When the vines have arrived on primitive worlds, they've taken over everything. Whatever lived there before was decimated. Our sensors show none of the original species. Those huge vines take over everything and wipe everything else out." Her shoulders sagged in a very human-like posture. "We never realized the vines were the brain of one huge plant creature and the little Botanist traders are part of it. We only knew that once it took hold, everything else disappeared. And the few times we sent ships to explore or try to help, they never returned."

Even better. The plant-things that had my people and my brother were world-killers as well.

"So why were you guys going to trade with them? What's so special that you'd do business with a bunch of murderers?"

Shiro grimaced. "We weren't sure the little guys were the same species as the vines. And they can make things no one else can." He gestured around the room. "The Siitsi are great scientists. My people are still alive because of our partnership. But they had an idea for something that would make life on my home planet a lot safer, and we needed seeds for a plant that didn't exist."

I remembered the little boxes they had been carrying after the trade. "So what did they make?"

A big sigh escaped Shiro's lips. "Dinosaur repellent."

CHAPTER 17

Shiro told me all about his home world.

How the Horizon Alpha made a rushed, disastrous landing on a planet full of dinosaurs. How they survived for three years, struggling against man-eating beasts from huge to tiny. How the whole world changed when the birdmen arrived.

"We knew they existed," he said. "We had their drawings, and we even had the body of the last one of them to try living on Tau Ceti e. But we had no idea they'd come back."

Tishi fluffed her feathers. "Our people received the beacon. We knew there was intelligent life new to the planet, so we sent a team to investigate."

She spoke as if she'd been there, but Shiro said this had all happened over twenty years earlier. "We have a mixed colony there now, with Siitsi and humans living together in a huge valley where most of the dinosaurs can't get in. My friend Caleb runs things, along with one of the Siitsi from that first shuttle. They're doing pretty well. You met Ricky last night, right?"

I nodded. He was the third human at the dinner table.

"Well," Shiro continued, "Ricky is Caleb's son. And these guys' parents are also on Tau Ceti e. Their generation is serving on Siitsi ships all over this part of the galaxy now. And the people who stayed on the planet are building quite a little city in the caves where they live. But there's still danger, and that's why we need the repellent plant. We traded for it with the Botanists, and now we're taking it back home to plant it all over the sides of the mountains where everyone lives."

So they did make it. The Alpha ship got safely to its destination. Well, not really safely, from the sound of things.

"Did the Beta make it?"

Shiro grinned. "Sort of. They didn't make it to their original destination, Omicron Eridani. Their ship was falling apart, just like yours. But they were able to land on Epsilon Eridani, and now you couldn't get a single one of them to leave for any reason."

"It's really something." Priya stood up and motioned me over to the aquariums at the back of the lab. "These crustaceans are native to the planet. The dominant species is a huge, intelligent insect that lives in giant hives. The insects eat these things, and the humans that landed there do, too."

I looked into the tank. The white crustaceans were larger than my fist, covered with pale armor plating. Long feelers waved from what I assumed was the front end as they scuttled around the rocks. *Who decided these gross things were food?*

"They carry a parasite," Priya continued. "A single-celled organism that uses the giant bugs as a secondary host. It lives in their brains and affects their sense of smell. Apparently, it's incredibly flexible and does the same thing to human brains. The people eat the crustaceans, and the parasite sets up shop in their heads. They smell things that non-infected people can't smell. It's how the insects communicate, and with the parasite on board, the humans can be part of the hive that way. Humans can't make the pheromones, but they can sure smell them."

Corey chimed in from behind me, startling me from staring at the nasty bugs in the water. "The queen of the insect hive secretes a special pheromone that bonds the other insects to her. They will literally die to keep her safe, and the humans that live there feel the same way."

From his seat at the table, Shiro added, "It's true. Once the Siitsi came to my planet and we had access to space again, we went looking for them. Since they weren't where they were supposed to be, it took us forever to find them. We just made contact last year, and we thought they'd be overjoyed to see us. Want to head out into space again, maybe find another place that wasn't crawling with bugs." He smiled. "Not one of them would even consider it. They looked at us like we had three heads. Their leader is a guy named Noah. They have hives all over the planet, with humans and bugs living together like a big, weird family. When we offered to bring them with us, you'd have thought we were offering to eat their grandmothers. They're so bonded to those bugs, there's no getting them off that world."

I shook my head. Hard to imagine living with giant bugs, especially if they looked anything like the nasty beasts in the tank.

"We've been studying the parasite," Priya said, gazing into the tank. "We think there might be some medical use for it." She pointed to a rack of small, silvery bottles next to the tank. "And we've been able to recreate the queen's pheromone as well. So far, our tests are showing that hundreds of species are susceptible to it. Once it gets into a brain, that pheromone is irresistible."

I picked up one of the small bottles, turning it over in my fingers. The liquid inside was slightly milky and swirled when I spun it around.

"It's a really interesting molecule," she continued. "When people with the parasite smell the pheromone or rub it on their skin, they're instantly bonded to the queen. But if you drink it, it's a sedative. Acts completely different internally. Strange. We traded a crate full of the waterbugs to the Botanists in exchange for the dinosaur repellent for the Horizon Alpha people."

Priya's words almost made me drop the little bottle. I shivered. Who knew what the Botanists could make from a parasite like that? I hated the Botanists for what they were doing to my people. Now I realized the danger went far beyond just my group of Delta survivors. They were a plague on the galaxy. The bottle fit nicely into the pocket of my borrowed pants. I wouldn't likely need a sedative, but so far nobody seemed to be on the same page with me about finding the Botanist ship and saving my brother. If I had to slip away somehow, it wouldn't hurt to be prepared.

I trudged back over and plopped down at the table. "So what do we do?" My fingers drummed on the surface. It had already been too long. "How are we going to rescue my people?"

Corey exchanged a glance with Priya. They both turned away from me, focusing on the bugs in the tank. Tishi pushed back from the bench and sidled over to join them. Only Shiro stayed facing me. He looked down at his hands for a long moment. The skin was dry and cracked. He looked very old to my eyes.

Finally, he lifted his head and met my gaze.

"Jonah, I'm really sorry. But there's no way to track them. No way to find them now." He glanced over to the door of the lab. "You're welcome to stay here and join the crew on this ship, or we can take you to either of the planets where the other Horizon ships landed."

No. Oh no.

His shoulders sagged, and his expression held a tired sadness. "I'm sorry, but your people are gone. There's no way to rescue them. You're the only survivor of the Horizon Delta."

CHAPTER 18

My fists slammed into the table, and everyone whirled around to stare at me.

"No! There has to be a way!" I felt heat in my face and water in my eyes. *It can't be true. I promised Shane I'd come back for him.* He was counting on me. They all were. If any of them were still alive.

"I'm sorry, Jonah," Shiro said. "I really—"

I cut him off. "Sorry? You're sorry? Look, I appreciate the rescue. I really do. But my brother is on that ship. And maybe twenty other people. We can't just leave them out there to die."

Tishi's whistles were translated into my ear. "It's not that we don't want to save them. But their ship is invisible. No one has ever found a way to track it." She waved a wing-like arm toward the outside wall. "It's out there somewhere, but we have no way of finding out where it is."

I jumped back from the table and stumbled over to the tanks. Corey and Priya backed away, leaving me alone to stare into the murky water. Everyone else made it. The other two ships. They were living happily on different worlds, and my people were dying, fed to a plant in the middle of a living, invisible spaceship. That was the end of the Horizon Delta. The hope of millions of people from long-dead Earth, sending out a ship full of lucky humans to find a safe place to live. That's what hope turned into. An acid pit in the belly of a fat, green plant.

Shiro's face reflected in the aquarium's side as he walked up behind me. He had a very slight limp I hadn't noticed when he was wearing the cloak and mask.

"I know how you feel," he said.

"You couldn't possibly know."

"But I do." He laid a hand on my shoulder, and I resisted the urge to pull away. "I was seventeen when we landed on Tau Ceti e. More than half of our people didn't survive the landing, and of those, more than half were eaten by dinosaurs before we finally found a safer place to live." His eyes were misty, reliving a troubled past. "I almost died more than once. I watched my friends die." His eyes grew darker. "I watched my father die to save my life. By the time the Siitsi arrived, I had no family alive on that wretched planet."

I shrugged. "But you had friends."

Yes," he agreed. "I still do. Some of them have kids on this ship. My own son is still there, and my daughter is an engineer on another Siitsi ship. I've been very lucky, and I know it's not the same. But I lost almost everyone. I know what it's like to want to save them and not be able to. I know how your heart breaks when you remember the people who died while somehow you lived."

Heat rose in my face again, and I pulled away from his fatherly arm. "But they're not dead yet. Not all of them. And we're just sitting here doing nothing." I had no idea what I wanted him to do. If the Siitsi in their fancy ship couldn't track the Botanist ship, why was I still insisting that something could be done? But I couldn't help picturing my little brother shivering in that cold, white hold. Waiting for the Botanists to bring in a vat of slime for him to eat. Huddled on the floor, trying to sleep. Waiting to see who they would take away next.

And when it was his turn? What would he think as they dragged him away? Would he be next to go, or last? Would he end up alone in that hold after everyone else was taken? They would come for him sooner or later. He might go willingly if he was last. Maybe he'd think they were taking him to be with the others that had disappeared and not returned. In a way, they were. They'd lead him down those blue-lit hallways. Into the huge room with the vines all around, blinking their lights as the nerve center of the ship that was alive anticipated its next meal. Maybe some of the little Botanists would look like people he'd known, as they used the DNA they stole from humans to make new buds, new Botanists. They might look more human, but they would never feel like a human. Never know sorrow, or shame, or regret for the life they destroyed. Up that ramp they would take him, whether pushing him or dragging him, or just opening the way. He'd look down into the giant pitcher, into the dark pool below him. Would they shove him off, or would he jump? Would the last human aboard the Botanist ship leap willingly into the darkness, just glad for the ordeal to finally be over? When next the horrible little green plants arrived on a trade moon, would some of them have his eyes? His nose? Would their faces squinch up in a lopsided grimace like he did when he was thinking hard?

"They took everything," I muttered. "Everything I ever knew." I pictured them puttering around the Horizon Delta shuttle that had been our final refuge when the giant, spaceborne ark became a dead hulk in the blackness between stars. "They'll use it all. Even our shuttle."

Shiro nodded, face reflected in the aquarium. "They will. But you're safe, Jonah. And that's a huge gift. You'll remember them, and they'll never be truly—"

He stopped speaking so suddenly that I tore my eyes from the bugs in the water. He had a funny look on his face, jaw pulled to the side in thought, just the way my little brother did.

"Their ship ate your shuttle."

I nodded.

"But it wasn't destroyed. They'll probably modify it and use it."

I nodded. "They had another one in the same hangar. The one that I hid on to get to the planet."

He spun me around by the shoulders until we were almost nose to nose. He had a crazy look on his face, eyes blazing with light.

"They have your shuttle. Every ship on the Horizon fleet has a beacon." He grinned, and I took a step back, alarmed by the intensity on his face.

"A beacon?"

He laughed. "A beacon." He glanced over at the Siitsi, who whistled in understanding. "A beacon the Siitsi can track. Jonah, I think we have a way to find that ship. There might be a way to find your people."

CHAPTER 19

We raced down the hallway together—me, three other humans, and a birdwoman who outdistanced us all, clicking along on her taloned feet. I lost track of all the turns we made, but eventually we entered a large room staffed by Siitsi and one lone human. There was equipment on every surface, holograms and flat screens showing images of what I assumed to be parts of the ship. Some kind of engineering space, I assumed. The quiet sound of Siitsi whistles and chirps came from some of the machines.

I suddenly felt incredibly alien.

This was their ship. Their language. Their technology, and their science. In the years since they had allied with the humans of Horizon Alpha, they had apparently made a place for our kind, but everything around me screamed that all the things I'd assumed my life would hold were gone. No matter what happened, if we rescued my brother or not, this was my life now. Forever an alien, no matter what world or what ship I lived on.

Shiro whistled to one of the birdmen, an aqua-colored male. The words translated into my ears, and the male cocked his head, listening. He turned back to his instrumentation and tapped on the panel. The hologram in front of him changed from an image of some part of the ship into lines of Siitsi language. His talons manipulated the data, and Shiro stepped back to where I was standing.

"It might take a little while to find it. Once they find the frequency, they'll have to figure out which one is coming from the Delta and which one is the shuttle. Should be able to tell from the movement, since the Delta is just drifting. And it might not even be possible. We don't know what their ship is really made out of." His face lost some of the hope that had blazed from his eyes. "It might block the signal."

My shoulders sagged. He'd seemed so sure.

"But if they find it, we can catch it?" I looked around the room from bird to bird. The intensity of the whole place had ratcheted up. Talons moved faster. The cacophony of whistles flew by too fast for my ear cuff to translate.

Shiro nodded, and Priya smiled.

"We have gravity propulsion," she said, eyes shining with pride. "The Siitsi have been working on it for centuries, and it's made us some of the fastest ships in the galaxy. If we can find them, we can catch them."

I had no idea what gravity propulsion was, but the question was obvious. "What if they have it too? If they're going a different way, they have a huge head start."

Corey sat down at an empty console. His fingers flew across the panel, calling up image after image on the screen in front of him. "I doubt it. No way to know for sure, but there are only a couple of species that have faster-than-light travel. Unless they stole it from someone else, I doubt they would have developed it on their own. They never seem to be in much of a hurry."

"That's true," Shiro said. "They don't need to be. Either they're heading somewhere to trade or they're heading to some uncharted world to take it over. They're like a flood, really. They don't have to rush."

I hoped he was right. *Go slow*, I silently willed them from across the blackness of space. *Wherever you are, just wait. We're coming.*

A quiet alarm jingled, and Corey smiled. "Okay, I have a reading."

My heart pounded. "You found them?"

He stared at his screen, Siitsi words and images flying across it at his direction. "Hang on. Needs to triangulate."

I held my breath for long moments while he worked. Priya stepped up beside me and laid a hand on my back. The touch of a human comforted me in that alien place.

"I think it's . . ." Corey's tongue stuck out the side of his mouth as he worked. "Okay. It's the Delta."

My chest deflated. Not the shuttle. Not Shane.

Corey's fingers flew over the panel. "Now that I know what to ignore, I can set it for a fainter signal."

I wondered how far he could scan. I wondered whether the beacon from the shuttle would ever be audible to whatever sensors on this ship were listening for it. I wondered . . .

"Found it!"

I pressed up behind Corey, looking for anything in the stream of scratches I could recognize. "Where? Where are they?"

He didn't answer for a while, working on his screen. "Hang on."

My hands were shaking. I couldn't stand still. I paced around the room, waiting for him to finish whatever calculations he was doing. Where was the shuttle? How far? How were we going to catch it? I rubbed my arms, stomping between rows of Siitsi in rainbow colors, all intent on whatever they were doing.

Shiro caught my elbow and guided me back to Corey's workstation. "Calm down. You're making me crazy, flapping around like that."

I stood still but couldn't hold still. My nerves were jumping. So close. So close to finding them. And then what? I had no idea. But Shiro would know. I was sure of it.

"Okay." Corey's word cut through my reverie. "I have them, and they're not too far yet. Heading out toward open space, but at their speed, we can catch them."

I whirled around to Shiro. "Okay then, what do we do? How do we rescue them once we get there?"

"First things first," he said and turned to Corey. "What's the heading? Where are they going? If it's toward a trade world, we might be able to beat them there if we really open up. Maybe set up some kind of ambush for when they land. If they're heading for a travel node, maybe we can get there first."

Corey's fingers slowed on the screen. He glanced back at Priya, and she peered more closely at the image in front of Corey. The back of her neck turned pink.

"Oh. They're . . . oh."

"What? What is it?"

Shiro and Tishi were also focused on the letters or numbers, or whatever was glowing in front of Corey.

Finally, Shiro muttered, "Oh, this is bad. This is very bad."

"What!" My shout made every Siitsi in the room pause. The clicking of talons all over stopped, and the chirping murmur died away.

Shiro kept his eyes on the screen, not looking at me.

"If the trajectory is correct, there's only one place they could be heading."

I waited for him to continue, pulse pounding behind my eyes.

"They must have sorted it out from the Delta. Or maybe they can access the computers."

My patience was almost at an end, but I refrained from grabbing him and shaking the words out of him.

"But I think it's obvious," he continued.

He turned to look at me finally, and his face held no expression.

"They're heading for Earth."

CHAPTER 20

I almost laughed.

"Well, they've got a surprise coming. Earth's not there." Relief poured over me, and all the tension in my neck flowed away. "They're heading for a big hole in space."

The look on Shiro's face silenced me. I glanced around the room. None of the Siitsi looked at me. They were all bent over their instruments, but no one was working. Even Priya avoided my eyes.

"What? What's going on?" It felt like that was the story of my life now, waiting to figure out what was happening.

Shiro straightened up. "Let's take a walk, shall we?"

I followed him out through the hatch, leaving everyone else behind. A million questions burned in my brain, but they all seemed ridiculous. Why would the Botanists go to a solar system that was basically empty? The whole Horizon project started when Mercury started wobbling in its orbit. Our scientists calculated that it would eventually fall away from the sun and head straight for Earth. Both planets would be destroyed by the collision, and the energy released would throw Venus right into the sun, and Mars right into the path of Jupiter. The chain reaction would destroy everything around our little star. It had all happened two hundred years ago. There was nothing but empty space there, and maybe a scattered debris field.

We trekked through the close hallways of the Siitsi ship. All my questions hovered on my lips, but I could tell from the set of his shoulders that there was no point asking Shiro. He'd tell me what he wanted to tell me on his own time. I'd learned that much already.

He waved a hand and a hatch opened before us. I stopped in my tracks, awed by the view in front of me. He ushered me into the room, and the hatch closed behind us, leaving us alone in a small, dark room.

"I come here to think," he said. "Magnificent, isn't it?"

And it was. The entire wall was a window looking out into the glory of space. No lights distracted my eyes from the glittering array of stars spread out before me. The entire bright swirl of the Milky Way shone in that window, and I was speechless at the beauty of it.

We had windows in the Delta. Tiny, thick-glassed portholes allowed us to squint out at the darkness. After so many years in space, they were cloudy and dim. But this was clear. The blackness between the stars was a perfect void.

In the dark of the room, Shiro guided me to a bench. I sat down next to him, awed by the spectacle in front of me. I knew the galaxy was huge. I had spent my whole life flying, then drifting through it. But I had never seen it like this.

He pointed, and I followed his finger.

"See that group over there?"

I had no idea which stars he was pointing to, but I nodded.

"That's Cetus. The constellation named after a whale by the ancient people of Earth. Tau Ceti is the star in the middle. It's where the Alpha landed. Where my son lives." He adjusted his point a tiny fraction. "And there, that's Eridanus. The fifth star from the bottom is Epsilon Eridani, where the Beta people live with their bugs."

I knew my constellations, and the groupings of stars looked nothing like what I remembered. "They're not shaped like I thought."

He dropped his pointing arm. "Not from where we are. Those stars are on the other side of the galaxy from us. Lucky for them." He pointed in the opposite direction. "That's where we all came from. Siitsi don't name the constellations like we do, and our sun wasn't part of any constellation humans ever named. It would look different depending on where you were looking from."

I strained to see where he had pointed. Which star was our sun? They all blurred together in my vision.

"There's nothing in that part of the galaxy. Where we are now, in this ship, we're part of the most populated area. You were heading for Chara, and it's a good thing you didn't get there, because there's not a habitable world in that system. Your descendants would have all died in orbit around a planet with no atmosphere. But there are a lot of worlds in this relative area. Lots of alien species. Some of them are friendly. Others . . . Well, you met the Botanists. Some are even worse than them."

The grandeur of the view was starting to wear off.

"So why does it matter if they're heading for where Earth was?"

He sighed. "Because it's still there."

Words failed me. I couldn't do anything but wait for him to explain.

"A couple hundred years ago, a lot of space-going species were just developing the grav drive. They tested it in what they considered to be an uninhabited part of the galaxy. It didn't work very well and sometimes played havoc with other star systems near it. Doesn't work like that anymore, but back then, everyone was making a mess of things trying to get it right."

A horrible thought dawned on me. "Someone did it? Someone pushed Mercury out of orbit?"

He sighed again. "I'm sure they didn't mean to. And who even knows what species it was? Everyone was testing their own versions all over the place. When the Siitsi finally noticed what had happened and went to investigate to make sure there was no civilization anywhere around, it was way too late. The Horizon ships were long gone. Earth was a disaster, and not just from the gravitational changes."

He lapsed into silence for a moment and I waited, still looking out at the black sky full of stars.

"All of Earth's hope rested on the Horizon fleet. When our ancestors left, there was nothing left for the rest of Earth's people to hope for. The planet had maybe three years left before Mercury was going to hit it, but all the cooperation the world had found to put together the Horizon fleet crumbled to nothing. Cities fell into chaos. What remained of governments fired nuclear weapons at each other. The weather was going haywire, with most of the Earth either too hot, too cold, or too underwater for people to live. Civilization as we think of it was destroyed, and hardly any humans survived.

"That's how the Siitsi found it. They'd improved their grav drive by then and stabilized Mercury and Earth back to normal. But it was way too late. The few humans that survived, under a million, were bombed and rioted and frozen and baked back to the stone age. No technology. They were hiding in caves and bunkers, and by the time they realized the planet wasn't blowing up, there was basically nothing left."

I could picture it. A wasteland full of radiation. "But some of them survived?"

He nodded. "Some did. They're primitive, but they're alive. The Siitsi have left them alone to rediscover what they lost. They're no threat to anyone, and there are no other inhabited worlds anywhere near them. They're safe." He grimaced. "They *were* safe."

"Why didn't the Siitsi help? If there were people there, why didn't they give them shelter or take them somewhere safer?"

Shiro's face looked blue in the dim light of the observation room. All the lines around his eyes were highlighted. He looked old and tired. "They have a lot of self-imposed rules for dealing with other sentient species. It would have broken their laws for them to interfere on the humans' home world. Even if they were helping."

"Why?"

"Years ago, when they were new to space travel, they found a planet of primitives. They were birdpeople of a sort, and the Siitsi were overjoyed. When the primitives started dying off in droves, the Siitsi realized they'd brought a disease with them, something the primitives had no defense against. More than half the population was wiped out. They made a law that they would never again set foot on a sentient species' home world. They sent their own beacons out to all the planets they knew about that didn't have sentient life, so that if another species ever colonized it, they could go meet them without endangering the world the colonists came from. It's how they found us. But they will never go to Earth. Not even to save it."

"But now the Botanists are going there." How could they not? However they figured out where we came from, they had found us, with our alien DNA. All the seeds we had in storage . . . How tempting to a species that lived for new life forms to assimilate into their own. The humans of Earth were sitting ducks.

"Humans are totally unknown to every other species." Shiro's words echoed the line of my thinking. "Earth is in a wasteland of uninhabited systems. Tau Ceti and Epsilon Eridani are far removed from everything else. Someday someone besides Siitsi will find them, but hopefully they'll be ready by then, and those worlds have Siitsi help. Earth doesn't."

I remembered the cloak and mask he'd worn. Pretending to be a birdman. "It's why you go out in disguise. No one else knows humans exist."

"Right." His eyes dropped away from the night sky. "They have your people. They're heading for Earth. If they get there, it will turn into another Botanist world, nothing but vines and plants. They'll destroy everything. And if they found it by analyzing data from the Delta's computers, the Botanists on that ship might even know where the Alpha and Beta ships went."

He finally turned to look at me. "They seem to be a secretive species. They won't have told any other Botanist ships about what they know. No competition from their own kind for the planets they want to colonize. But Jonah," he said, eyes boring into mine, "if we don't stop them, it won't just be your brother and your friends that die.

"It's every single human in the galaxy."

122

CHAPTER 21

I don't care about Siitsi rules. We need to get my brother back, and we need to protect Earth."

Shiro shook his head. "It's not that simple. This is a science vessel. We don't have weapons to blow something like that out of the sky, even if we could see it, which we can't, and even if we wanted to, which we don't, because there are humans on board. We've got explosives, but not torpedoes or laser cannons or any of the kind of thing you've seen in movies."

My shoulders slumped. Of course I didn't want to blow up the Botanist ship. Not until our people were safely off it. But then . . . yeah, he was right. I envisioned firing huge cannons and watching it explode in a big, green flash, with plant parts drifting out into space. Now that I thought of it, even that probably wasn't a good idea. Plants could grow from cuttings. With my luck, we'd blow it up, and a little piece of that vine would float down to some other world, grow up, and take over ever everything. But still. I had hoped.

"So what do we do? We just . . . leave them? Go back to Tau Ceti or wherever you were heading when you found me? Just let my brother die?" My face was hot, hands shaking. We couldn't. No way I was leaving them. But what could I do? Once again, I was captive. This time it was humans who wanted to help and birdpeople who didn't want to eat me, but I was as helpless as I'd been on the Botanist ship.

"Look, I don't like it either," Shiro said. "Every human is precious now. We don't have anywhere near enough for a stable population on either of the planets we've colonized. Even twenty more healthy people would be huge." He sighed. "But I don't know any way to rescue them."

"You have to. You're captain of this ship, aren't you?"

His eyebrows shot up. "Captain? Hardly. I'm just security around here. Siitsi ship, Siitsi captain. She's already been informed, and we'll stay close if we can find them. But that's the best we can do."

Not good enough. "Can't we call for help? Aren't there other ships around?"

He nodded. "There are other species all over this part of the galaxy, but none of them would likely assist, and we don't want any of them to know Earth or the colonies are so unprotected. And there are other Siitsi ships, but nothing in communication distance." He pointed out the window again. "See that star?"

Which one? "Sure. I see a lot of stars."

"That one is three hundred light years away. But the space-going species have set up travel nodes all over this part of the galaxy. They're like . . . tunnels. You go in one side of a mountain and come out the other. But instead of a mountain, it's hundreds of light years of space. With travel nodes, we could reach that star in a couple of months."

I nodded. Wormholes and star gates were a staple of my sci-fi childhood.

"But there are no nodes anywhere near Earth because nobody ever goes there. We set them up near enough to Tau Ceti and Epsilon Eridani for our own use, but those nodes are secret. Only Siitsi know where they are. No beacons on them. We can travel in no time where there are nodes, but without them, we can't go faster than light speed."

"Can the Botanists?"

He shrugged. "I doubt it. We can send unmanned drones out faster than light to set up the nodes for travel, like a relay, but I don't know of any species that could get to Earth in less than about sixty years. This ship can't get there at all. It's not a long-haul vessel."

"Then we get a long-haul vessel."

That might help Earth. But it wouldn't help my brother. Even if the Botanist plant didn't eat him, he'd be almost seventy by the time they got to Earth. I'd be well over eighty. Not much good for a rescue.

"Can't. We can travel through the nodes, but we can't communicate over those distances. We're on our own."

My fingers found the chipped edge of the bottle in my pocket and traced the sharp edge. "So that's it. We just abandon them."

Shiro's expression darkened from sadness to anger. "We don't have any choice. I guess their ship can just fly there, and plants don't care how long it takes. They probably took on enough food at the trade stop to last them the whole way.

They're probably able to photosynthesize, so they wouldn't actually need much. Just starlight to keep them going, or maybe they can even go dormant like a tree in the winter. Who knows?" He rubbed a spot on his leg. "I don't want to abandon anybody. Believe me. There was a time I thought I'd been abandoned by my friends. Almost died."

"So you know what it's like. What my brother must think." My voice broke. *He must think I died trying to escape. Because he knows I'd never give up. And yet, here I am.*

"Don't you think if there was a way we could—"

His words were cut off by a chirp from the panel at the door to the room.

"Shiro? Come back to the workshop." The voice was Corey's coming through the panel.

Shiro spoke into the air, not bothering to turn around. "What is it? Did you find something?"

The voice echoed off the huge glass window. "They're changing course."

CHAPTER 22

We raced back through the corridors. By the time we reached the giant room full of Siitsi and their working displays, I was clutching my chest and heaving for air. Shiro wasn't even winded.

"What? Where are they going?" He was talking before the panel was fully open.

Corey sat at his station, and Ricky—the other guy I'd met the night before—was standing over his shoulder. Priya wasn't there, but Tishi was. Her feathers were fluffed with some emotion, though what it was, I couldn't say. Her eyes looked wild, though.

Ricky nodded to Shiro and me and returned his gaze to the screen in front of Corey. "They've made a slight adjustment to their course. They're not heading straight for Earth anymore, though there isn't much on their direct line now."

Shiro pushed past me to stare at the screen. The array of symbols and diagrams meant nothing to me, so I hung back.

"Why did they turn?" Shiro reached over Corey's shoulder and manipulated the panel. New symbols appeared, scrolling up past the old ones, still incomprehensible.

"We're not sure," Corey said. "There are no inhabited worlds that we know of on this trajectory. They're still basically heading for Earth's zone, but . . ."

"What's this?"

I followed Shiro's finger. More symbols.

Corey peered closer. "It's a system, for sure. No known habitable planets. Hang on." He worked the panel for a few tense moments.

Ricky leaned in. "There's a system. Couple of planets around a red dwarf."

I knew that was a kind of star. Small and relatively cool, they could burn almost forever, but they were nowhere near as hot as Earth's sun.

"Could one of them have life on it?" I asked. "Could they be going to take it over?"

Corey shook his head. "There's only one planet close enough to harbor any kind of life, and it's tiny. Hang on."

His fingers flew over the panel, changing the screen image. It pulled up a diagram that I could finally recognize as a star with four planets. There were Siitsi symbols all around the chart, but of course they meant nothing to me. *I guess I'll have to learn their language. One way or another, I guess I'll be living with them somewhere.*

"Look here," Corey said, gesturing to the screen. "This planet is dead. But it has a moon." A small, round body came into view, orbiting the second planet out from the red dwarf star. "It's incredibly cold, but I'm getting readings of an atmosphere. Oxygen-poor, and not fit for humans. Way too cold anyway. But it looks like that's where they're going now."

I turned to Shiro. "Then that's where we have to go. Whether they're landing there to set up a new home or just—I don't know—stopping for whatever reason. It's our chance to catch them and maybe rescue my brother."

Shiro nodded, eyes still on the screen. "How cold?" The question was for Corey.

"Minus three hundred, give or take."

My eyes bulged. Minus three hundred degrees?

"That's maybe . . ." Shiro thought for a moment. "Would be about minus fifty degrees Celsius. Minus sixty Fahrenheit."

Did the Botanist ship have heat? Could plants survive that cold?

"Can people live in that temperature?" *Surely not.*

"For a very short time, yes," Ricky said. "With proper exposure suits, maybe a couple of hours."

My people were wearing what they'd had on when the Delta was breached. Light pants, long-sleeved shirts. The kind of shoes made for a people that would never set foot outside in their lives. So far that was true for all of them except me.

I nodded. "And are there 'proper exposure suits' on this ship?"

Shiro put a hand on my shoulder. "Look, we're not going down there . . ."

I cut him off. "You can do what you want. I'm not asking anybody to go with me." My eyes returned to the image on the screen. It had changed from a line drawing to what looked now like a live video. Were we close enough to see it? How close did a ship like this have to be to get an image like that? The moon was white, covered in clouds. Here and there the clouds cleared to reveal what looked like sheer ice in ripples that might be mountains or deep valleys. What could the Botanists want there?

"Nobody's going anywhere," Shiro said, but again I cut him off.

"Yes, they are. My brother is going there, whether he wants to or not. If they land that ship, I'm going down there and getting back on it. One way or another, I'll find a way to get my people off, or maybe I won't. But either way, I'm not abandoning my brother to those plants."

Corey and Ricky stared at me.

"You can't go down there. You can't even think you're getting back on a Botanist ship." Corey's mouth hung open.

Ricky's eyes sparkled. "No, you can't. But we could get a lot closer. No one has ever seen one up close. We could at least follow them to that ice moon. Get some images of their ship. Just think what we might be able to learn, even just from seeing the thing up close."

I sensed my ally. "Right," I said. We could maybe . . . I don't know, orbit that moon for a little while. Just have a look. We'd be the only ship that ever saw one and came back to tell the tale. You'd be famous."

Shiro's hand on my shoulder squeezed tighter. "Right. Just orbit around it. Get some pictures. Just look."

He sees right through you. Not very hard, really. I hadn't exactly been secretive with what I wanted since they brought me on board.

But Corey either didn't hear the sarcasm or ignored it. "If the ship can manipulate the wavelengths it absorbs so it's invisible, it will probably look white on an ice world. Even just seeing that would go a long way toward finding some way of tracing their ships when they don't have one of your shuttles inside."

Your shuttles. Not ours. Yours. He wasn't born on a Horizon ship. He had no idea what it was like. But for all I knew, he might have been born on this one.

"And maybe," I continued, "if they land there, we could take a shuttle down and get a sample. Like, cut a piece away to study it. You have shuttles that could do that?"

"Oh, yeah." Corey was hot on the idea. "We have a couple of tiny ones in bay six they might not even notice. With full exposure suits, we could land somewhere nearby, maybe around one of these mountains." He pointed to the ripples on the ice world. "There would be time to get around it and maybe—"

Shiro cut him off. "Nobody's going down there. We can orbit and take a look. Get your images. But nobody is taking a shuttle anywhere." He glared at all of us. "We do not land; we do not explore; we do not get a sample of anything. Is that understood?"

Corey's face fell. "Yes, sir."

Everyone answered in the affirmative, and even Tishi's chirp sounded dejected.

"I've got work to do," Shiro continued. "Ricky, can you take care of Jonah today? Maybe get him some clothes that fit?"

He nodded. "I'm off here in half an hour. I'll show him around."

Shiro gave my shoulder one last squeeze, turned, and stalked out of the room.

I eyed the image of the ice world, spinning around the dead planet somewhere in space.

I'm coming, Shane. I don't know how, but I'm going to get you back.

CHAPTER 23

I hung back from Corey's station. He and Ricky huddled together, whispering over the image. I pretended to be absorbed in my own thoughts, but my gaze never left the spinning moon below.

Finally, Ricky straightened up and turned to me. "Are you ready for some lunch? Then we can take a tour if you want." He glanced back at Corey's workstation and shook his head. "Botanist ship. Can't believe we're so close."

"Sure," I answered. "Lunch sounds great."

We left Corey still huddled over his screen and padded down the long hallway. I was trying to put together a mental picture of the ship as we walked, and asked what I hoped were innocent-sounding questions.

"So how many levels on this ship?"

"Thirty-two," Ricky said. "Most of it is either science labs of one kind or another or crew housing or engineering. The Siitsi home world is super crowded and apparently kind of a mess, environmentally. Most of them left it hundreds of years ago. They tried to spread out all over their side of the galaxy." He waved a hand to the left, apparently the direction "their side" was on. "But most of the worlds they found weren't hospitable. A lot of their population lives on ships like this now. Some of them live on the dinosaur planet where my mom and dad live."

Even in my plotting, that sounded intriguing.

"It's really dinosaurs?"

He grinned. "Sure is. Well, sort of. They're not really the same as Earth dinosaurs, but some of them look pretty dead-on. I was born there, but as soon as I turned fifteen, I was history. Joined the Siitsi crew to train in biophysics. I study stress in biological systems."

I snorted. "Stress? I guess I'm a perfect research subject, then."

He laughed. "Well, not really that kind of stress, but yeah, for sure." His face got serious. "I really am sorry about your family, by the way."

"Thanks."

We entered another elevator. I was starting to recognize some of the symbols labeling the corridors and elevators. This one was two vertical slashes with a single diagonal line connecting them. Kind of like a very shaky letter N. I had no idea what the symbols meant, but at least they were looking familiar. I could pick a few of them out now.

"How is that possible, though?" I asked as the elevator moved silently. "How are there dinosaurs on different worlds? And people that look like birds?"

"Panspermia," he said. To my confused look, he added, "It's a theory that all life all over the universe developed from one single cell and was carried everywhere on comets and meteors, or just flying through space, seeding the universe with the same basic building blocks. In theory, dinosaurs, or things like dinosaurs, could evolve on different worlds to look similar, if the conditions they developed in were similar."

The word sounded vaguely familiar, and the theory made a weird kind of sense, especially considering all the species I'd seen on the trade world. They all breathed the same kind of atmosphere I needed to survive. They looked different, but there was nothing that didn't look like it could possibly have evolved on Earth, given different circumstances. Different dominant species. No asteroid that killed our dinosaurs, or no ice age, or a million different things that shaped the animals that lived on a planet. *Or the plants. Don't forget the plants.*

We entered the dining hall, and he indicated a seat for me. In a few minutes he returned with different fruits and a warm, sweet drink that tasted a bit like honey.

"So how long until we're in orbit around that moon?" I didn't look at him when I asked it, focusing on my lunch.

"Couple of hours," he answered. "Don't know how long we'll stay. Assuming they're landing their whole ship, as soon as it moves, we're not staying around. No way we want to get swallowed like you did." He grimaced. "Sorry."

"It's okay." But it wasn't remotely okay. *Patience. A couple of hours.*

"What was it like? Inside their ship?"

I told him everything I could remember. The light that came from everywhere and nowhere. How the vines felt under my hands when the lights chased through them. The smell of the giant pod that ate our people. He hung on my words just like I was clinging to every new thing I learned on the Siitsi ship. When we finished our meals, we dropped the dishes off on a cart pushed by a small Siitsi who stared at me, chirping happily. My cuff didn't translate anything, so I smiled in what I hoped was a friendly way. The little bird's eyes got round, and it flitted away, rolling the cart full of dishes.

"So what do you want to see first?"

I pretended to consider a moment. "That shuttle I rode in on was cool. Can I see the shuttles?"

"Absolutely!"

Along the way I asked him to point out the scratches that were Siitsi language. "How do you know which ones are numbers and which ones are letters?"

He shook his head. "You're thinking like a human. Their language isn't anything like ours. For us, each syllable comes from letters put together to make a sound. Theirs is more like the writing of the old Earth Chinese language, where each stroke in a symbol contributed to the overall meaning of the symbol. A line might tell you how it's pronounced or what it means or how it relates to the next character. It's like that because their language is not really made of words like ours." He thought for a moment. "I wonder what kind of language the Botanists use? Did you see any writing anywhere in their ship?"

I shook my head. "I'm not sure they have writing, or any kind of language. Not like Siitsi. Can you teach me anything? Like, what's that say?" I pointed over a closed hatch.

"That's a four," he said. "Down, up, down, up." It looked like a capital "W." He pointed to the number on the opposite wall. "That's the three. Down, up, down." Like a backwards "N."

I looked at it. "So a five is down, up, down, up, down?"

He laughed. "No. It's a single down with a hash across. Like that." The next doorway was marked as such. Sort of like a plus sign.

The door opposite would be a seven, then. A backwards "N" with a hash across.

I hoped we'd go into six, which was surely the door on the left, marked with what looked like a "V" with a horizontal slash, but instead he took us into five.

It was a huge hangar with one giant shuttle in it.

"Can we look inside it?"

"Sure."

The shuttle's entry hatch was open, its ramp extending onto the floor. No one else was in the bay, and I hoped that was normal when the ship was in flight. No reason to be around the shuttles when there was nothing to land on. We trooped up the ramp and into the big, open cargo bay.

"Are there space suits in here?" I tried to sound like a little kid.

"Right in here." He showed me a small door next to the one I assumed led to the cockpit. I waved my hand in front of the small panel, but it didn't open, and Ricky didn't open it for me.

"Here's the cockpit." The door slid silently open with a wave of his hand.

Inside the cockpit was a total mystery.

"How do you start it?"

"Mostly automated," he said. "That pad turns the whole thing on, releases the gravity grips that hold it to the floor, and signals to the big bay doors to prepare to open."

The buttons and panels were all labeled with Siitsi writing. *Did you expect an owner's manual in English? An illustrated guide to flying an alien shuttle?*

Ricky was obviously proud of the technology, and I kept playing the "awed little kid" role, which wasn't all that hard.

"I bet it takes years to learn how to fly one. Maybe someday I could be a pilot, too."

He smiled and pointed at a couple of long, thin rods protruding from the panel. "It's not as hard as you'd think. The pilot steers with those, and when the shuttle's sensors detect ground, it lands automatically."

I touched a hand to the steering rods. *You're insane for even thinking this.* "That's really cool. Are they all smart like that?"

"Everything about a Siitsi ship is smart," he replied. "Ready to go see the engine room?"

A huge yawn escaped me, and I pretended to stretch. "Actually, I'm still pretty wiped out. Is it okay if I go back to my room and get a nap? Maybe pick it up later?"

"Sure."

On the way back to my room, he chatted on about his time with the Siitsi and the science he was working on. I'd mostly been pretending to need a nap, but the droning science lecture had me yawning for real by the time we reached my room.

"Oh, here," he said. "Let's get the panels to recognize you, since you're staying at least a while." He pressed his hand to the panel and made a Siitsi whistle. "Now press your whole hand there."

I did, and he nodded. "Good. Now all you have to do is wave, and anything that's not restricted will open for you. Just talk to the panels, and you can ask for directions. Your ear cuff will translate."

He left me and I waved my hand to close the door.

Inside the room alone, I sat on the edge of my bed.

138

Totally insane. You can't fly a bird shuttle. But no one else was going to help. In a couple of hours, we'd be in orbit around an ice moon, with the Botanist shuttle on it. My only way back to my brother. *You'll die trying.* But I was all right with that. I wasn't okay with living and not trying.

Just a couple more hours, Shane. I'm coming.

CHAPTER 24

There was no clock in my room, and even if there had been, I couldn't have read it. The numbers hadn't made sense to me when Ricky explained them, but I saw the six. The small shuttles were in bay six.

I rested for what I thought might be a little more than an hour. The voice in my head went round and round.

You're never even going to get it to fly.

If you do, you'll never even find the moon.

If you do, you'll never find the right place to land.

If you do, you'll never land it safely.

If you do, you'll never survive the cold to get to the Botanist ship.

If you do, you'll never get on board.

If you do . . .

I stopped there. The idea that Shane might already be dead—that they all might—I couldn't even let the thought turn into words. He had to be alive. And I had to save him.

When I thought enough time must have passed, I used the little bathroom and crept out of my room.

Walk normal. Don't sneak. Look like you're supposed to be here.

Two wrong turns made me backtrack. When I passed a human, I nodded, keeping my eyes down. My oversized pants bagged around my ankles, and the shirt was rolled up at the sleeves. But the boots fit me well enough, and I tromped down the halls until I found the elevator.

Hadn't thought of that.

There weren't any buttons. Everyone else just whistled at it. And I wasn't sure what floor I was going to.

"Shuttle hangar six," I said, hoping there wasn't any kind of voice-recognition software analyzing my tone to hear the shake in my words.

The door slid closed and the elevator moved. I sighed and leaned against the wall.

My stomach growled. *Should have stopped for a meal.* How long did it take for a shuttle to reach a planet? An hour? Two? Ten? How long 'till I reached anywhere with food? *You're not going to. You're going to crash in flames. Or freeze on an alien moon.* I dug my fingernails into my palm hard enough to quiet the doubts. *Doesn't matter. I'll find Shane or die trying.*

Would it matter, though? If I died trying to rescue him, he'd never know. I could just as easily stay here on this comfortable ship. Go live with the dinosaur people, or learn how to speak bird and fly around the galaxy. Shane wouldn't know either way.

But I would.

HORIZON DELTA

The elevator door slid open. I retraced my steps from earlier in the day with Ricky. A few Siitsi passed me, walking faster than me on their long, backwards-bending legs.

Stealing their shuttle. Very heroic.

But they had more. They wouldn't miss it.

Down the hallway. I guessed the single slash down was bay one. The distance to the next set of doors told me that it was a huge hangar. Was there just one huge shuttle in there, or a bunch of smaller ones? There was so much I'd never know.

You could. You could stay here.

But the words in my head were drowned out by the words in my memory.

Don't ever give up hope.

It's what I'd said to Shane when I left him in that livestock hold. How many days ago? I refused to think about it. He was alive. He had to be. And I made him promise not to give up hope. He'd hold onto that hope until they dragged him out of the room. Until they shoved him down the corridor. Until they pushed him up the ramp. Until they tossed him off into the pool of acid in the mouth of the Botanist pitcher. Until the acid dissolved him into the tiny molecules they would use to make more moving plants to take over some other planet, filling it with grasping vines and silent, staring pods.

He would never give up on me. So I would never give up on him.

Down the hall. Four. Five.

I waved my hand in front of the door to bay six.

It opened.

I glanced both ways down the hall. No one in sight, human or Siitsi. I stepped through the door, which closed behind me.

The bay was smaller than the one Ricky had shown me earlier in the day. Three small shuttles sat side by side, noses pointing in, away from the huge, closed hatch on the far wall.

You're going to have to back it out.

I didn't even know how to fly it forward.

You're going to crash it right here in the hangar.

Maybe I was. Rescue Shane or die trying.

Which shuttle to take? They all looked the same. All of them had open hatchways with extended ramps. I decided to take the one on the far left. There was a little more room between that one and the one in the middle. At least if I wrecked it, I wouldn't take out all three of them.

I trooped up the ramp. Inside was a small cargo bay, maybe big enough for thirty people to sit on the floor. Forty if they stood up. There weren't more than twenty, maybe twenty-five, people left on the Botanist ship when I left it. There would be fewer now. Plenty of room for everyone. *When you back out of here and fly down there and walk across the ice and get in another shuttle and fly to their black bean ship and find them and rescue them and fly back down to the ice planet on their shuttle. Jonah, the hero.*

Jonah, the dead man.

I waved my hand in front of the little door to the cockpit. A clanking sound behind me froze my arm for a moment.

Someone's here.

Diving into the cockpit, I hunched down in front of the pilot's seat, curling into a ball.

Footsteps on the ramp.

A rustling and swishing sound from the little cargo bay.

I peeked up around the seat.

Shiro stood there with a long, white exposure suit draped over each arm.

"We'll need these once we get there." He eyed me with a shake of his head. "And move, kid. You're in my seat."

CHAPTER 25

I pulled on the exposure suit over my clothes. Baggy and wrinkled, it was a big one-piece jumpsuit with attached gloves and a hard ring that clicked around my neck when I zipped it up the front with a plastic fastener that wasn't really a zipper. It sealed me in, and Shiro showed me how to use the buttons on the neck ring to make a thin, transparent helmet come out of it and wrap over my head.

"All the tech is in the ring," he said, manipulating the panel in the pilot's dashboard. "It makes oxygen and filters breathing waste. This is the simple kind, just designed for quick outside work. It will keep us warm and breathing for a while once we land."

I settled into the co-pilot's chair and watched him power the shuttle up. Alarms sounded in the bay around us.

"What's that noise?"

He touched the panel again. "Warning that a shuttle is taking off. The hatch behind us is about to open right to space. Best if no one without a suit is caught walking around the hangar."

Right.

There was no rearview mirror, but one of the screens in front of me showed the view from behind. The huge bay door opened to reveal black, starlit sky outside. With a small lurch, our shuttle lifted off the hangar floor and backed away from the others. Small windows on each side showed the door to the hangar passing by, then the huge outside of the Siitsi ship as we pulled out of the hangar. I watched through the windshield in front as the hangar door slid shut, and Shiro spun us around, facing away from the ship.

Just black sky. I wouldn't have had the faintest idea where to go.

The artificial gravity kept me in my seat, and I felt us nose down. Shiro manipulated the panel and the long steering rods to pull us around under the giant ship. A small gray circle appeared in my view.

"Is that the moon?"

He shook his head. "It's the planet. The moon is on the other side of it. There's no way we can really hide once we're on the other side of the planet, but at least they won't have as much visual warning if we come from this side."

I thought about that. "Probably not looking visually, though, are they?"

"Nope."

Who knew how the Botanists scanned for other ships? Maybe we would get incredibly lucky and find that they relied on their own ship's reflective cloaking ability to keep them safe. Maybe they weren't scanning for approaching ships at all.

Right.

"They're plants, though," I said, continuing my thought aloud. "So maybe they'll be dormant in the cold? You said it's an icy moon?"

"It won't be cold inside their ship," Shiro answered. "But I doubt they're expecting trouble." He nodded to a little door behind our seats. "We've got some weapons in there, and I packed some explosives in the back. If we have any kind of surprise on them, we might not die immediately."

A dark chuckle rumbled from my throat. He knew we were going to die on this mission just like I did. But he came anyway.

"Why are you here, Shiro?"

His eyes closed for a moment as we flew.

"A whole lot of years ago, I did something stupid. Just one missed step that took me out in the middle of a dinosaur jungle. The rest of the guys on my team had to leave me there. No choice at all. I couldn't walk." He was rubbing a spot on his leg, almost reflexively. "I made them leave me because trying to drag me along would have killed all of them, along with everybody else that was depending on them. They said they'd come back for me."

I waited for him to continue.

"It didn't look good." He glanced over at me. "Dinosaur jungle and all. I was dead meat out there, literally." His hands gripped the steering rod. "But they came back. I was almost gone, washed up on a riverbank, totally broken. But Caleb came back, just like he said he would. None of the other soldiers survived. Nobody knew where I was. Nobody else on that planet would have ever come for me. But Caleb came back."

He understood. Shane was waiting for me. He believed it just like I did. He knew we would almost certainly die trying to save him.

But once upon a time, someone named Caleb came back for him.

"Thanks, Shiro." There was so much more I could have said, but everything I felt was in those words.

"You're welcome."

We flew in silence. The gray planet grew in the front view screen, and when we veered around it, a small, white moon appeared ahead of us. It was half shrouded in darkness from the angle of the star that was its sun.

A planet. A moon.

On my years aboard the Horizon Delta, we had passed a lot of stars in the distance. But we never got close enough to see a planet as more than a tiny, glowing dot in the sky. There were asteroid fields and meteors, but nothing like a real world.

On the way to the trade moon, I'd been sealed in a filthy box. When I emerged, I'd been too panicked to revel in the feeling of an actual world beneath my feet. But now, here it was.

We passed the planet on my side, and I watched its rocky gray surface roll past. Dull and dead, it was still the most fantastic thing I'd ever seen. As we approached the ice moon, it revealed itself to be full of mountains and crags. Long shadows from the angle of the sun made it dappled white and gray on its light side, and the dark side was a rippling black sea.

HORIZON DELTA

"Where are they parked? Can you tell?"

Shiro was watching one of the screens in front of him. "I was assuming they'd keep the big ship in orbit and send a shuttle for whatever they're doing on the moon's surface. But I'm tracking the beacon on the Horizon shuttle. It's parked on the planet, but faint, partially blocked."

The shuttle bucked as we neared the moon's atmosphere.

"I think they landed their whole ship down there," Shiro said. "I'm coming in from the dark side. The scan shows they're parked at the side of a mountain right at the twilight line. I'll come in low and land us on the far edge of it. We'll have a little walk to get to it, but if they're not scanning for us, they might not realize we've landed so close."

I gripped the edge of my seat against the bumping of the little craft. Fire filled our windows, the burn of entering an oxygenated atmosphere.

"How likely is that? Them not looking for us?"

He shrugged, knuckles white on the steering rods. "Not likely." A grin split his face. "But that's kind of my specialty. The world I'm from, nothing is ever easy, and every morning might be your last, in an ugly, bloody way." He turned and winked at me. "Maybe this is our last morning. But Horizon soldiers don't go down without a fight."

The fire cleared, leaving the moon's dark night around us and a shadowy surface below.

"I'm not much of a soldier," I said. "But those plants took my people. I didn't ask for this fight, but one way or another, I'm going to finish it."

We bounced through the sky toward the icy mountain in the distance.

The Botanist ship was on the other side. My brother was in that ship.

Hang on, Shane. Two Horizon soldiers are coming.

CHAPTER 26

Shiro pulled off a clean, soft landing. We were in darkness, shadowed by the mountain. It ended abruptly to the right of our shuttle, dropping off to a smooth, icy surface that was probably a frozen lake or ocean.

"How far to their ship?"

He checked the screen. "About five kilometers around the side of the mountain. Won't be a pleasant walk."

The ship powered down, leaving only a dim glow inside. Shiro said, "In a ridiculous show of optimism, I'm leaving some power going and the heat on in here. I'm sure we'll be coming back here with a bunch of cold, rescued humans. They'll appreciate not getting into a freezing ship."

He stood up and I followed him around behind our seats to the little door he'd showed me before. Reaching inside, he pulled out a couple of guns. They were dark green, with two handles on the bottom, a shoulder strap, and no visible trigger.

"Here. Hold this in both hands."

I wrapped my gloved hands around the handles, and he touched a spot-on top of the weapon.

"It's biometrically attuned to you now," he said. "Won't fire for anyone else." He pulled two more guns out of the alcove. "The Siitsi aren't killers, and these don't shoot bullets. Just a shockwave, so they will probably only stun the Botanists, although it's possible the force of the stun might be too much for the little ones. The field is pretty wide, so just aim and squeeze on the front handle. Hope for the best."

He slung the other two over his shoulder, and we trooped back into the cargo hold.

A large white bag sat strapped to the floor.

"Explosives. Just in case."

He unstrapped the bag and slung it over his other shoulder.

"I can carry some of that," I protested, but he shook his head.

"I'm fine. You just carry your own gun and be ready for whatever happens."

We stood near the back hatch and touched the spot on our neck rings that made the thin helmets wrap around our faces. Shiro reached over and touched another spot-on mine, and his voice echoed in my ears through some kind of comm system.

"You ready to go out there?"

I nodded. The helmet moved with me.

With a quiet swish, the hatch slid open and its ramp extended. Cold air blasted in, and a small rumble vibrated through my neck. The suit warmed a bit, but the chill was already settling in.

Even if we find them, they'll die out there.

"How are we going to get them back here without them freezing?" I asked as we descended the ramp.

Shiro's voice in my helmet said, "Hoping there will be some kind of exposure protection in their ship we can use. I have a couple of extra suits in the bag." He hitched up the white bag on his shoulder. "But if there's more than five of them, we'll have to figure something else out."

Five suits. That's all he expected to find alive in there. Five. *One of them has to be Shane.*

The helmet protected my ears from the whipping wind that buffeted me as I hiked along the smooth ice. Nothing moved in the darkness.

"How does this moon have an atmosphere?" I knew there was oxygen here. Not enough to live for long, but enough for the mad dash between ships I'd imagined myself doing after I crash landed the shuttle here.

"The Siitsi say there's a lot of photosynthetic bacteria living in the ice here," Shiro said. "The atmosphere is really thin, but it might thicken up in another couple million years, warm this moon right up. Come back in a few million, this place might be a tropical paradise."

We trooped on. The suit protected my skin, but cold seeped into my bones. I started to shiver and walked faster. Without the suit I would have died in minutes out here. How something so thin was keeping me warm enough to live was another Siitsi mystery.

The end of the Botanist ship came into view around the side of the mountain. It was the first good look I'd had.

In space, it had reflected black. Here it was stark white. A huge, smooth, round bean, with just the back edge visible. It wasn't as big as the Horizon Delta. But it was easily as big as the Siitsi ship we'd left. Big enough to swallow Horizon's shuttle. Big enough to swallow fifty Horizon shuttles.

We crouched down, staying close to the sheer cliff wall next to us. It felt stupid to be creeping along the ice. If they had any kind of sensors deployed, they would know we were here. More of their enormous, smooth craft was coming into my vision in the dim twilight. The sun was either rising or setting in the distance, but we were in the ship's shadow.

A rushing gurgle was getting louder in my ears. We bent low and scuttled around the back of the Botanist ship. It sat right up against the cliff wall, sitting right on its rounded bottom. No landing gear, no wheels or feet. Just a giant white bean on the solid ice.

"Which way?" I whispered.

Shiro peered down the cliff side of the ship. No doors. No ramp. No windows. Nothing on this side that would let us get inside.

I hadn't thought of that. It had just swallowed our shuttle out in space. Corey had wondered if the whole thing was some kind of rudimentary life form, able to bend its shape as necessary, opening and closing its hull at will, like some kind of soft putty. What if we couldn't get in?

Shiro motioned for me to follow, and we scuttled around the back toward the light of the sunny side. It was getting brighter by the minute. Sunrise, then. Not sunset. It hardly mattered. The whole moon was nothing but ice. It wasn't going to warm up for another few million years.

The rushing sound got louder as we traversed the huge end of the Botanist ship. I'd called it the back end, but with an oblong bean, who knew?

HORIZON DELTA

My fingers and toes were numb. The helmet kept my face from freezing, but my body was weakening in the deep, painful cold. We had to find a way in, and soon. If we spent much more time out here, the rescue would be over before it began. Even now I realized this had been a one-way trip. No possible way I could make the long hike back to the Siitsi shuttle and its heat. Even if we gave up right now, we would die in the cold shadow of the mountain.

Bright sunlight blinded me as we crept out from under the white bean's backside. The Siitsi helmet immediately darkened to compensate.

Shiro stopped and turned to face me. "Look," he said. "I know you want to rescue your people, and so do I. But if we can't get them out, we're at least going to save what's left of the people on Earth." He hitched the bag of explosives on his shoulder. "If we can't get inside, I'm going to blow up as much as I can of the hull and hope to cripple the ship. No matter what, we can't let it leave this moon."

Under my feet, the ice was vibrating. I looked down the long, bright length of the ship's side. A thick tube extended from the ship like the stem of a huge mushroom. It dipped into a pool of liquid water with thick ice rimming the edges of the tiny churning lake.

"How is that not frozen?" I asked.

"The tube must be melting it," Shiro said. We huddled under the edge of the ship for a moment, watching it. The water was bubbling all around the edge of the tube.

They came here for the water. Of course they did. The realization hit me. They were plants. They might live off photosynthesis from distant starlight and gain some nutrition from the living things the pitcher swallowed, but in the end, they were plants, and plants needed water to survive. They were preparing for an extended space flight to Earth. The Botanists were stocking up.

The edge of the tube stuck out from the side of the ship. We sidled closer to where it came out, edging along until we were standing underneath it. Shiro looked up.

"It just sticks straight out. Can't see a way in."

But I did.

The tube was long and narrow, plunging into the churning water. Shiro wouldn't fit through it.

I would.

"Is this thing waterproof?" I held the gun up in shaking hands.

Understanding dawned on his face.

"Yeah, but you can't—"

Before my courage could desert me, I plunged into the water, leaving Shiro in mid-sentence. The icy water compressed my suit around me, shocking my already-cold body into near-paralysis.

Gripping the gun to my chest, I kicked over to the edge of the tube and pushed my head under the water's surface.

The sides of the tube ripped past my shoulders as I was sucked up into the Botanist ship.

CHAPTER 27

I clenched my arms around the gun, shocked into a frozen statue as the water pressure shot me up the inside of the tube.

Time slowed down. I had enough time to wonder what would meet me at the top of the tube. A filter that would stop my body as the water rushed by? It wouldn't take long for me to freeze to death. The helmet over my face would keep me from drowning, but the cold would kill me in short order. Would it lead into some kind of thresher, designed to rip up any solid chunks of ice that were swept up the suction tube? Was I a fraction of a second from being ground to bits?

Jonah, you're an idiot. Shiro risked his life to get you here, and you just jumped right into—

The tube spit me out into an open pool of water. I clawed my way upwards, bouncing into the sides of a tank with ice water churning all around me. Upwards? Was I sure this way was up? The cold slowed my arms and legs, the weight of the gun around my neck pulling me down.

Down. The gun pulled me down.

I pushed off what must be the bottom and flailed at the water.

My head broke the surface.

I was in a large, dim room, bobbing in a huge tank, flowing in the current toward . . .

Oh, yeah. There's the ice crusher.

The tank funneled down a short river toward a series of thin slits in the mouth of a large tube. Great hunks of ice had been shoved up against the slits, and as I watched in horror, giant spikes closed in all around the tube, crushing the ice into tiny bits that flowed away into the slits.

I slapped my arms against the flowing water, cold forgotten as adrenaline shot through me. The edge of the tank was smooth and white, and the force of the current dragged me down toward the ice crusher. My gloves slipped on the edge.

This can't be it. This can't be the end. I'm so close.

Desperately, I clawed at the smooth sides, rocketing closer to the deadly tube entrance. A huge chunk of ice floated past and I kicked at it, trying to lunge over the side, but only succeeded in shoving it past me, bumping down the narrow space.

My head bashed against the side, and I flipped over on my back, the weight of the gun strangling me as it pulled down on my neck, still sliding toward the slits.

Gotta get a grip on the edge. But it was wet and frosted with ice. My suit-covered boots slid off the side, and the edge was too thick to wrap a hand around.

My feet bumped into the giant ice chunk and my body slammed to a halt. The ice was sucked up against the slits, and my boots slid on its surface. Any second the huge spikes would chomp in from all around, crunching the ice and my legs.

I shoved off the still piece of ice with all my might and grabbed for the edge of the tank. With a scream of effort, I threw my right arm over the side. My boots slipped on the iceberg, and a deep grinding sound rippled through the rushing water all around me.

The spikes descended.

With one huge pull, I heaved half of my body over the edge. The spikes ripped into the bottom of my boot, shredding the suit as they crushed the ice I was pushing against. Freezing water poured up my leg.

I threw my leg over the edge, hauled with the last of my fading strength, and flopped over the smooth ledge. There was a momentary sensation of falling, then the air left my lungs in an agonizing whoosh as I crashed to the floor.

★★★

My leg was numb. Dazed and frozen, I rolled to my stomach and pushed up onto all fours. My lungs burned for air, and I grabbed at the neck ring of the suit. The helmet slipped from my face, retracting into the neck ring. I pulled down the front of the suit and wriggled out of it, gasping for breath. The suit hung around my frozen leg, but I lacked the strength to kick it off.

Rushing and grinding noises echoed in the large room. Was it attended? Were little green Botanists coming even now to drag me away? I tried to lift the gun, but still couldn't breathe.

Rest. In and out. There's air here. It's warm.

I sat back on my heels, head lowered onto my chest, pulling in great heaves of the warm, humid air. Finally, I felt strong enough to stand, leaning against the wall of the water tank next to me. My feet slipped in the wet pool of my splashing escape, but I was able to get a hand onto the top lip and haul myself up. I peered over the edge into the tank. Ice water flowed by. The teeth of the grinder chewed and retracted. But I was out. I was alive.

Get out of here. Find Shane.

I stumbled out of the puddle, kicking off the shredded bottom of the suit. My boot and pants leg were soaked, but tingling pain was returning to my frozen ankle.

How long did I have? How long would the ship stay parked here, sucking up water for the trip to take over Earth? How long had it already been here?

How long till Shiro gave up on me and blew the ship up from the outside with us still in it?

I had to find my people. Find a way out. Find Shiro outside and get back to our shuttle.

The sound of rushing water filled the room as I staggered away from the tank. A bright rectangle of light drew my eyes to a far wall. Open doorway. Like a moth to a flame, I plodded toward it.

Through the hatchway, a long corridor stretched away. There were closed doors on each side, and I had no idea where it led, but Shane and the others weren't in this damp room. They must be somewhere above. My footsteps squished on the slick floor.

Down the hallway to a T junction. Which way? To the left was another closed door. To the right, another long hallway and at the end, the bottom of a ramp leading upward. I turned right and started down the hall.

Behind me, doors slid open.

I whirled around, raising the gun.

More doors hissed open all around.

Little green walking plants closed in from every side.

I squeezed the front handle of the gun, spraying its pulse in quick bursts. Botanists flew into the walls.

With a roar of rage, I spun around, sending the hated green aliens into wet splats that slid down the walls and collapsed twitching onto the floor.

"We're humans!" I screamed. "Not livestock! Humans! And we have guns!"

The remaining Botanists backed away into the open doorways all around me. I turned to race for the ramp.

Above my head, large pores opened in the ceiling. Red-tinged gas billowed out.

I had time to think, *This ship really is alive; it's all one giant plant*, before the gas reached my nostrils and everything went black.

CHAPTER 28

"Jonah? Jonah, please wake up."

My head felt like lead. My eyes were glued shut, nostrils packed with dripping snot. The inside of my mouth tasted like burning fuel and every part of my body was on fire.

"Jonah?"

A voice penetrated my clogged ears and I forced one eye open.

Shane crouched over me, his little face creased with worry, cheeks streaked with tears. When he saw me open an eye, he flung himself on top of me, crushing the breath I was still struggling to draw. With a grunt of pain and effort, I managed to lift my arms and wrap them around him. He hitched in my arms, great wet sobs rocking through him.

"I'm here," I croaked. "I'm okay."

Someone peeled Shane off me and pulled on my shoulders until I was sitting up. I coughed and spat, wiping my eyes and face on the long tail of my shirt. It was still damp, so I couldn't have been out for long.

"Where have you been all this time? Where did you get those clothes?"

I looked up, eyes wobbling into focus.

Six faces looked down at me. One was Shane. Mrs. Lucien from the Delta's kitchens was there, and Mr. Conrad, my math teacher, along with three others whose names I couldn't recall in my fuzzy, addled state.

There was no reason to ask where I was. The smell of the livestock room flooded into my head. I had a moment to wonder if everything I'd been through was just a dream. Had I really left this ship? Escaped and found humans and birdpeople, and returned to rescue everyone? Or had I just fallen asleep here and dreamed myself a hero? *Some hero.* I looked down at my legs. The baggy pants Shiro had given me were held up by the belt I'd worn on the Siitsi ship. The gun was gone, of course, but everything I remembered was real enough.

Shiro. I left him out there to freeze to death. Would he wait out there for me? Find another way in? Or did he have the sense to realize I was dead the moment I hit that water, and use his remaining strength to get back to his warm shuttle after he blew up this ship? For his sake, I hoped so. He'd gotten me here and I'd botched it. Looking around the room at the puzzled faces surrounding me, I realized I might as well have never left. All my travels had accomplished nothing. We were all going to die here, in a ship full of plants bound to destroy the remains of human life on Earth.

"Help me up."

They hauled me to my feet, and I stumbled over to the water trough. A shiver ran down my arms as I plunged my hands in, drinking deeply of the warm, tasteless water. My stomach growled.

"Do they still feed you algae?"

Shane shook his head. "You've been gone for days. Where did you go? Did you find the others?"

I nodded. "There's another room like this one. A couple of days ago there were eleven people in it. By now, who knows?"

The thought of not telling them anything more crossed my mind. It wouldn't ease their minds to know there was a rescue ship out there in orbit full of bird people that weren't coming to rescue us. That the other Horizon ships had landed on other planets and had colonies that were thriving, or at least surviving. That although the people of the Delta were doomed, the human race lived on and still would for a while after the Botanists destroyed Earth, a planet we had assumed long gone for two hundred years.

But at least it was a story. I wouldn't tell them about the fate that awaited those that were dragged out of here. Wouldn't have Shane's last days filled with nightmares of the acid at the bottom of a pitcher, the central brain of a plant ship, with vine nerves spreading all through its living hull. I hoped that none of the ones with human faces had come into this room. In the days I was gone, they must have assimilated more and more human DNA. The way they plugged themselves into the vines, the ship's brain that led to the pitcher in the center, they must all have bits of human swirling inside them by now.

My thoughts were interrupted by the hiss of the door sliding open. Three Botanists pushed in a low cart full of multicolored squares. None of the Botanists had a face I recognized, and they didn't bring a vat of algae that I could try to hide in.

167

The food was tasteless, raw crunchy bits of something they must have extruded based on the DNA from the seeds they stole from the Delta.

"Don't eat the brown ones," Shane advised. "They aren't poison, but they do a number on your belly."

Trial and error. Maybe the brown bits were made from the seeds of a pine tree. Something we could plant on a new world but couldn't eat. I chose a handful of orange thing. Carrot. *Back to my roots.* I snorted at the ridiculous joke.

When the Botanists came and wheeled out the food cart, I eyed the open doorway. Three more of them stood just outside in the hallway, aiming their weapons in at us. It would be suicide to rush them.

It hardly mattered. Die now, or die later. At least I had a bit of time with Shane.

I turned to him and grabbed him, hugging him until he squealed.

"I missed you so much," I murmured into the top of his head. "I told you I'd come back."

He peeled my arms off and stepped back, grinning at me. "I knew you would. I told everybody you'd never leave us even if you could."

My throat tightened. *I would. I did.* I swallowed hard. *But I came back.*

I checked his wrist, and the swelling had all gone down. It seemed like forever since he sat on the med bay table in the Delta, crying about the injury. We sat on the hard ground, and I started my tale.

"So I rode the cart into the other room and found the rest of our people." *Well, not all of them. Skip over that.* "And they wheeled me out and I ran down the halls until I found our shuttle." *Skipped over quite a bit there.* "They were coming, so I hid in a crate inside the other shuttle, that big one we saw when . . ."

My words were cut off by the opening of the door.

Four Botanists strode into the room. We all scrambled to our feet and stood with our backs against the far wall. I held Shane's hand, and his shivering raced up my arm.

They walked down the row of us. All of them had guns. They weren't here to feed us this time. They were here to feed one of us to the pitcher.

All of them looked more human than the last ones I had seen. None of them wore a recognizable face, but the shape of the heads and hands was more familiar. They were using us. Learning from our bodies. The little group stopped in front of me and reached out.

They grabbed Shane.

He screamed as they tore him from my grasp.

"No!"

I lunged forward, throwing myself at the two that were dragging my little brother. I kicked at them, knocking them away.

"Get off him!" I shouted, arms and legs flailing.

Shane stumbled away and they grabbed me, one on each limb, lifting me off the ground as I struggled. Strong arms bound my hands in front of me and threw me to the floor.

Shane made a dive, but they pushed him away.

"No, Shane, don't!" I cried. "You can't—"

One of the Botanists cracked me in the head with the butt of his weapon. The white ceiling swirled around me as they dragged me from the room, the screams of my brother cutting off with a hiss as the door snapped closed behind us.

CHAPTER 29

I didn't fall unconscious. The blow to my head dazed me, but I was awake as they dragged me down the hallway. Past the door I knew led to whichever of our people were left. Past other closed hatches where strange, alien howls told me that more livestock awaited a fate they couldn't possibly imagine.

My hands were bound in front of me, and they dragged me by the legs. The smooth floor was a gift; at least my aching head didn't bounce on an uneven surface. I worked my wrists against the bonds as I slid on my back down the hallways. How long did I have? The memory of my furtive creep through this ship seemed like ages ago. The ropes they used—or vines, or whatever they made on this hateful vessel with the stolen DNA of countless worlds—held fast. It had a tiny bit of stretch, and I thought that with enough time I might be able to wiggle free.

And then what?

They had guns. They were strong, and although Priya had said the brains in these individuals were rudimentary, connecting to the controlling brain of vines and the pitcher plant nerve center when they plugged in and went dormant, there was nothing stupid or clumsy about their movements. On my very best day I might get lucky in an unarmed fight against one or two of them. But there were four touching me right now, and countless others stalking the endless corridors of the living Botanist ship.

We didn't cross over the catwalk that passed above the factory floor where they extruded everything they needed, and all the things they made to trade with the fools of the universe who had no idea these cute little green men were one with the terrifying vines that took over and destroyed worlds. Perhaps they wouldn't care. Humans had always been willing to look the other way if it meant getting what they wanted.

My head cleared with every step they took. I managed to work the restraints halfway down my left hand, where they squeezed my fingers until they were almost numb. Another few minutes and I might pull free. If only I had the Siitsi gun . . . but I'd had it when I boarded. Didn't do me much good.

I'm sorry, Shane. I failed you. Failed us all.

In a way, I was so much luckier than everyone else on board this vessel. True, I was about to die just like the rest of our people, and countless others. My body would be broken down in the pitcher and used to strengthen the Botanists in some way. Some distant world might soon be trading with a small green man wearing a Jonah face. But I had seen so much more than anyone on the Delta ever imagined.

I was born on a generational ark in what should have been the middle of its journey. My feet were never supposed to walk on a planet. My lungs were never meant to breathe non-recycled air. My eyes should never have seen a sunrise. I was destined to be a forgotten ancestor, someone to be considered fondly once a year when some distant, future relatives gave thanks for those that made the journey, appreciated for the sacrifice of my boring, predictable life. My existence was only meant to continue the human species, bound for a time when the Horizon Delta found its home and my far-off descendants stepped out onto a safe world to start new lives.

When the Delta broke down, even that noble cause was lost. I was just supposed to die in space. In a strange, unimaginable way, I was about to do just that. The fact that instead of sending my DNA forward into a new future for humans, I was sending it out in a Botanist ship to destroy the remaining humans on Earth . . . well, that was just a further insult.

They dragged me on through the hallways and up a long, curving ramp. I knew what was at the top.

But I had seen so much. A trade planet full of strange, frightening creatures that thought I was a food animal. Friendly aliens with bird beaks and an unpronounceable language. Humans from other worlds. Sunrise over a moon made of ice.

And I hadn't even gotten to tell Shane about it. He would have loved it, even though he would never have believed me. He'd have thought I made it all up, a crazy tale to pass the time, just like on the Delta's shuttle in those awful days after our parents and almost everyone else had been killed. Felt like a million years ago.

The ship rumbled. Was it Shiro's explosives? Was this it? A sudden sense of movement swayed through the floor. No, not an explosion. A launch.

Must have sucked up enough water. Time to fly to Earth.

They turned a corner and we passed through a small room. Boxes and crates were stacked along both sides. My view from the floor showed alien writing on crates made out of strange, foreign materials. At the bottom of one of the stacks, I saw the tubs the Siitsi had traded with this ship on the day Shiro rescued me. The writing looked almost familiar now. What had they been trading for? *Dinosaur repellent.* That's what Shiro had said. Some kind of seeds that would grow into a bush with a smell or chemical that would keep dinosaurs out of the valley where people and Siitsi lived together on a far-off planet.

The floor rocked under my back. The huge, living bean ship was airborne, blasting off from the ice moon toward an Earth with no possible defense.

A hatchway hissed open.

The dim light of the room was filled with flashes from all corners. Above me, thick vines crawled up the walls and across the distant ceiling. Blue lights shot through the vines, messages flowing up and down the nerve center of the ship. The room tilted, and I slid to the side as we passed through the hatch. The giant bean ship was airborne. Shiro's explosives must not have worked, or maybe he didn't have time to set them. I hoped he had gotten back to his shuttle before the thing took off.

A smell of acid hit my nostrils, and we approached the bright cone of light shining down into the middle of the room.

This was it. The pitcher awaited.

I kicked out as hard as I could, throwing the Botanists off my legs. After the long, docile drag through the hallways, they were unprepared for the sudden movement, and my legs were suddenly free. I flipped over onto my belly and pushed myself up with hands that were almost free of the stretchy binding.

Botanists from all sides converged on me. Small green hands, tentacles, pincers, and suckers grabbed my legs and lower arms.

"Okay, okay." I stopped struggling. It was futile. "But you're not dragging me. I'll walk like a human." I glared at them. "That's what I am. A human. A thinking, feeling, living—"

They cut my monologue short with a shove. My words dissolved into grumbles.

With a jerk, my left arm came free. I held it in front of me and worked the bindings off my right. It wouldn't do any good, but at least they wouldn't throw me into the acid pitcher trussed like a hog for slaughter.

Straight ahead, the ramp loomed up. Botanists surrounded me. I shuffled forward, propelled by their momentum.

Goodbye, Shane.

Goodbye, Shiro.

Goodbye to all the humans on the Siitsi ship. And all the humans I'd never meet on the dinosaur planet. I'd really wanted to see that one.

Goodbye to all the humans living in harmony with the giant bugs. The ones whose brains had turned to mush from the parasite in the water bugs and the pheromone the bug queen used to rule them.

All around the huge chamber, blue light winked faster through the thick vines. The pitcher was hungry. Excited about its meal.

When is the last time it ate? What was it? One of my people? The water bugs traded by the . . .

Water bugs.

My free hands felt for the heavy weight in my pocket. I reached inside, fingers feeling for the chipped corner on the thick silver bottle.

All that human DNA. The Botanists must be full of it by now. Rudimentary brains. And a parasite that lived in the water bugs. A parasite that in insect and human brains made the producer of pheromone in my pocket into a beloved ruler. Bugs and humans would die for their insect queen.

I was out of time.

The edge of the ramp gave way to the long drop. I peered over into the gaping, acid mouth of the pitcher.

Please work. Please work.

I whipped the bottle from my pocket and held it overhead, ripping the seal off the top. I couldn't smell a thing, but every Botanist near me went still, frozen green statues fixated on the bottle in my hands.

"I am your king!" I shouted, my words echoing in the huge, silent room. "Obey me, and free my people!"

The Botanists inhaled.

It's working. They're listening. They have to do what I say.

"You will take us to—"

They lunged toward me.

The bottle flew from my hand.

Together we watched it tumble over the edge of the ramp, droplets flying as it plunged into the waiting pitcher mouth below.

CHAPTER 30

From every corner of the room, Botanists charged. They popped off the vines where they had been dormant and raced toward me. The ones on the ramp lunged forward.

I tried to dodge out of the way, but they were everywhere, tumbling up the ramp in droves, little green bodies like a river flowing uphill.

A handful of them went over the edge into the pitcher. More barreled up behind me on the ramp, and I grabbed at anything I could—slimy heads, slapping tentacles, sharp pincers. It didn't matter. The force of the Botanist flood pitched me off the front of the ramp and into the spiked mouth below.

I scrambled for the smooth, round upper edge of the pitcher and got a single hand on it. My boots landed on a pile of Botanists, and more rained down from above, careening off me and into the acid depths. Inward-pointing teeth all around the inside of the tall pitcher poked into my skin as I clung to the side, feet slipping on the writhing bodies underneath me. The smell inside burned my eyes, and thick bile bubbled up in the back of my throat. The golden cone of light from above shone down, throwing everything around me into crazy, spiked shadows.

This is it. It's swallowed us all.

The entire plant rocked all around me. More Botanists piled in from above, bouncing off my arms and shoving me into the teeth of the pitcher.

I kicked at the Botanists under my heels, and acid splashed all around us. My left hand was digging into the slippery ring around the top, and my right flailed around, trying to grab at anything that wasn't a sharp spike, or the continued rain of Botanists from the top of the ramp, impossibly far away. Beneath me they scrambled, kicking up more acid.

My legs burned, and my pants were shredding away in the chaos. Drops of acid ate into my boots from all directions, and I kicked frantically, scrambling for purchase against the slippery sides.

More Botanists tumbled in, and my fingernails scratched away the rim of the pitcher.

My grip let go.

I flopped down onto a pile of writhing plants. There was no time to think. No time to react. The slimy, acid-coated creatures roiled around me until the cone of light from above was obliterated by all the bodies inside the pitcher.

With a sickening shudder, the pitcher exploded.

Botanists from all around the outside tore their way in, ripping at the thick green walls, shredding the spikes in their frenzy. Along with the other Botanists trapped inside, I spilled out onto the floor in a slimy plop.

Every single one of the little green monsters scrambled to get back in.

I rolled away, tearing at my acid-soaked sleeves and pants legs, which fell in hunks off my arms and legs. My boots flopped on burning feet, and my skin was on fire in angry blotches all over. I crawled under a vine and peered out at the chaotic scene.

Blue lights shot up and down the woody vines, and the whole ship vibrated under my hands and knees. Hatchways opened all around, and more Botanists poured in from every side, leaping over the vines and their slower brethren to attack the shredded remains of the pitcher.

One of the Botanists emerged from the pile of thrashing bodies, holding aloft the silver bottle I had dropped into the spiked hole.

Twenty more dove on top of it. Bits of green plant flew everywhere.

The ship shuddered. All around the floor, Botanists tore each other to shreds, lost in the chaos of destruction, each one ripping apart anything with a trace of the pheromone on it.

They shredded the slimy sides of the pitcher. They flung themselves onto each other. Tentacles, pincers, and flat, lily-pad feet flew up from the melee. The smell of wet, green pulp mixed with the acrid acid stench that clung to me.

I stumbled to my feet and pushed my way through a hoard of Botanists, all racing into the room to throw themselves onto the remains of the pitcher. The hatch to the storage room was open, and I sprinted through it and down the hallway.

Botanist guns, empty crates, and all manner of debris littered the corridors. They must have literally dropped everything as the pheromone wafted through the ship.

In bugs and humans, the pheromone made its subjects adore the queen.

Apparently in the rudimentary, human DNA-infused brains of the Botanists, it ignited a single-minded frenzy. They would stop at nothing to get to the drops of scent. They would rip each other apart to find it.

I raced down the halls, struggling to remember the path they had dragged me down. The remains of my boots flapped around my feet, and I stopped for a second to kick them off. The farther from the pitcher's room I got, the fewer Botanists I saw. I paused to scoop up one of their guns from the floor. Sooner or later the pheromone's power might wear off.

The ship bucked and shook under my feet. Its brain, the great green pitcher, was dead, ripped to shreds by its own living buds.

How long could it fly with no brain? I envisioned it crashing back to the ice moon, splitting open on its surface. Or maybe we had escaped its atmosphere and would drift forever, just like the Horizon Delta.

The rumbling growl of the thrusters hitched. For an instant, my stomach lurched as the floor stopped pushing on my feet and the ship's momentum faltered. It roared back to life and I stumbled, catching myself against a wall.

I careened around a corner and ran straight into three small Botanists. They were milling around in a circle, clearly confused and directionless as the ship shuddered around them, dying as the last of its pitcher brain fell to pulpy bits. One of the Botanists was the many-legged one I called Spider the first time I saw it.

A few drops of the pheromone must have dribbled onto my shirt when I dropped it. I was hardly wearing any of it anymore, with both sleeves hanging in burned, torn shreds around my arms.

They froze, turned, and attacked.

CHAPTER 31

I raised the gun I'd grabbed, but couldn't find a trigger to fire it. Instead, I bashed at them, hurling their bodies off me. They fought without direction, just flinging themselves at me. I kicked and spun, wielding the gun like a club. Spider was the last one standing, and I smashed the gun into its face full of eyes. Legs flailed and green goop splattered everywhere. In moments, all three of the Botanists lay motionless on the floor.

The ship's momentum hitched again. My stomach lurched as we lost gravity for a longer second. The Botanists and I floated up a hand's length from the floor before the thrusters kicked in again and the floor jumped up to meet us.

Footsteps pounded down the hallway. I spun around, gun raised like a baseball bat.

Shiro burst into view, heavy bag slung over his shoulder, gun aimed straight at me.

"It's me!" I screamed. "Don't shoot!"

He slid to halt and eyed the dead Botanists around me. "Wow. You look like a war zone. What happened?" His Siitsi uniform was wet, and slime dripped from his hair.

I looked down at my arms and legs, bleeding and burned under the tattered remains of my clothes. "I had a run-in with a pitcher and some acid. How did you get in here?"

A look of disgust made his nostrils flare. "Cut a hole in the side and squeezed right in. It was trying to heal itself all around me. Got stuck inside the wall and had to just keep cutting. Never smelled anything like that in my life."

I grinned and lowered my gun. "The ship is dying. I poured the bug pheromone into the pitcher and they all went nuts, tore it apart." *That was it. Poured that pheromone on purpose. That's what I did. Totally knew what was going to happen.* I held out my arms with the shreds of my shirt clinging to my bloody skin. "Fell in. Got out. But the ship is in a bad way. We keep losing thrust. I killed it, and when it goes down completely, we'll fall out of the sky."

"Time to go, then."

He turned to head back the way he came, but I didn't move. "We have to get my brother. There are people here. I need to be with Shane when we crash."

"Crash?" Shiro smiled. "Who's crashing?"

He grabbed the smallest of the dead Botanists, throwing the floppy body over his shoulder. "Where are they?"

I ripped away the remains of my shirt and dropped it, leading the way down the halls until we reached the panel. It didn't open to my touch, but Shiro slapped it with the dead Botanist's hand, and the door hissed open.

Shane and the others rushed forward. He threw himself into my arms and I winced as he clung to my abraded skin.

"It's okay, buddy," I murmured. "I'm here now."

He looked up at me, tears in his eyes. "What happened to you?"

The rest of the captives crowded around us. "What's happening? Why is the ship shaking like this?" They stared at Shiro. "Who is . . . ?"

Shiro shook his head. "No time. Gotta go."

We rushed down the hall to where the rest of our people were held, and I stopped at the door. "Here! There are more in here!"

He used the Botanist's hand, and eight more people joined our sad parade. They were full of questions, hanging in the doorway as if we were Botanists in disguise.

"What's going on?"

"Where are we going?"

"Who's that man?"

They barely had a chance to gape at the stranger. We didn't pause to answer their questions, just motioned them to follow.

I made Shiro stop at some of the other doors, and we let some of the other alien livestock go. Some of the beasts were small enough to carry, and others we herded ahead of us. The ones that rushed the doors, snarling, we left behind, closing the hatchways as they lunged for us. Shiro finally dropped the dead Botanist and we rushed down the vibrating corridors.

"Where's the shuttle? The Horizon shuttle?" Shiro's voice cut through the rumbling all around us.

A giant lurch spilled all of us to the ground.

"Come on!" I struggled to my feet, pulling Shane up with me. "This way!"

The slick covering on the walls of the corridors started to wrinkle as we ran. The blue-green surface streaked with brown around the edges, our feet leaving squishy marks. The ship really was dying. Shriveling up like the dead plant it was.

Groups of Botanists fell to Shiro's stun gun. I looked up to the ceiling, but no pores opened. No gas escaped. The ship had no defense. And in a very short time, it wouldn't matter as it splattered all over the ice moon with us inside it.

We burst into the huge hangar. On the far side, our shuttle had listed to one side, the floor giving way under it.

"Everybody in!"

Our frightened people herded the animals onto the shuttle, beasts crashing over the rows of seats.

Shane held back from the ramp, last to get on. "I was so scared. I thought they had you."

I crouched in front of him. "They couldn't hold me. Not when I had a little brother to save."

He scuttled into the ship, and I closed the hatch behind us. The smell inside the shuttle was worse than I remembered from our long days adrift. Terrified cries from humans and other creatures filled the hold.

The Botanist ship's pulsing engines cut out. We lost gravity and everything inside and out of our shuttle floated free. People and alien animals rose up around the seats, screaming and bleating with terror.

"Everybody hold onto something!" I yelled.

I clawed my way forward, pulling myself hand over hand across the rows of seats until I reached the cockpit and hauled myself through the open doorway.

Shiro was strapped into the pilot's chair, flipping the

switches that made the shuttle roar to life. "What's happening? Did we leave the atmosphere?" My voice was raw in my throat.

"Maybe," Shiro said. "Or maybe we're still in the moon's gravity. If everything in here is falling at the same rate, that's the same as no gravity at all. No way to know from inside."

"Can you fly this thing?" I pushed myself off the ceiling to reach for the back of the copilot's chair next to him, settling onto the seat and belting myself in.

"Why not?" He shrugged. "How hard can it be?"

He switched our shuttle on. Thunderous engine noise filled the hangar as the Botanist ship plunged into darkness around us. Our shuttle's running lights illuminated the damp, browning walls trapping us inside.

"There's no hangar door," I realized. "It just opens to swallow what it wants. How are we going to get out?"

Shiro gripped a long handle, lowering the thrusters to a growling idle.

"Wait here. Keep everybody inside."

He unstrapped himself from the seat, grabbed the bag that was floating free behind his chair, and shoved his way back to the main shuttle hatch. I followed him, bouncing off people and animals in the hold, and shut the hatch behind him to keep everyone from floating away. I managed to haul myself back to the cockpit in time to see him attaching the explosives he'd brought from the Siitsi ship along the wall in front of our shuttle. There were only four little silver blocks, and he checked a small remote before returning to the hatch and locking it. He pulled himself into his seat beside me and belted in.

"Might want to shut your eyes." Shiro's hands were white-knuckled on the remote.

The ship rocked with the strength of the blast.

I opened my eyes to see a small, smoking hole in front of our shuttle's nose. Through it streamed bright, white sunlight.

Sunlight, not black sky and stars. *We didn't make it out to space. We're in the atmosphere. We're falling.*

"What's our altitude?"

A grim smile from Shiro. "We'll find out."

The shuttle leaped forward as he gunned the thrusters. It lurched toward the hole in the side of the ship, grinding its nose into the small hole, which already looked smaller than when the explosives opened it up seconds before. The brain of the Botanist ship was dead, but the side was still trying to close up around us, whatever cells in the walls that were still alive struggling to heal the hull as they'd been programmed to do.

"Punch it, Shiro!"

The hole peeled wider with the force of our thrusters grinding us through it. I could see out the windshield. Sky. And horrifyingly close below us, solid ice.

"Go! Go! Go!"

Thrusters screamed. With a great, sideways heave, our shuttle tore through the shuddering hull and soared free into the bright afternoon sunlight.

Jagged spears of ice thrust up right below us. "Too low! We're too low!" I shouted.

Our little ship groaned as its belly sheared off the tops of the ice shards below us, scraping against the top of a frozen mountain. Shiro gunned it and we lurched into the sky. He pulled us around in a wide arc to see the enormous, shuddering white bean of the Botanist ship smash into the side of a giant glacier. It burst into a million pieces, sliding down the solid white cliffs.

HORIZON DELTA

A cheer erupted from the people pressed against the shuttle's windows.

Shiro turned the shuttle away from the crash, and we descended through the clear blue sky toward a smooth lake of ice below.

CHAPTER 32

Shiro hadn't told anyone what he was doing when he left with me on the shuttle. Sometime during our rescue mission, his crew must have realized we'd taken it and where we had gone. The Horizon Delta shuttle we used to escape from the Botanist ship had no way to dock with the Siitsi ship, and there wasn't room on our small, borrowed Siitsi shuttle for our people and all the terrified alien animals we had rescued on our way out. So we parked our Delta ship on the ice and waited for the Siitsi to come.

"They'll be here any minute," Shiro said. "No way they can possibly resist a chance like this."

Shane was glued to my leg, and we all crowded together in the cockpit, away from the animals crashing around in the passenger area. We barely had time to tell my story to our baffled, shell-shocked people before the Siitsi arrived. They landed right next to us, and we herded the animals into the cargo hold of the first shuttle. The Siitsi pilot squawked her indignation as her hold was filled with screeching, baying creatures, but she flew them on up to the mother ship and sent another shuttle for us. We dashed across the small patch of ice, hurling ourselves into warmth and safety.

We stayed in orbit around the ice moon for over a week as the Siitsi scientists salvaged all they could from the wrecked Botanist ship. The Siitsi buzzed with each new piece brought on board. The frozen samples they retrieved might help them figure out the secrets of the plants that could make anything from nothing, and the vines that could kill a whole world. One day the science discovered here might protect other worlds when living Botanist ships came to colonize a primitive planet.

When they had everything they wanted, we left the system and headed for the Delta, drifting in space.

The trip only took a couple of hours. Our people were still wary of the Siitsi after only a week on the ship, but Mrs. Lucien had already started poking around the kitchens, and Mr. Conrad was learning Siitsi numbers, working with their mathematicians. The feathered females doted on Shane, who was already speaking a few words of their language.

They'll be all right. Humans are a hardy lot.

When we reached our destination, all of us filed into the observation room, looking out the huge glass wall. Everyone gasped as I had at the magnificent, star-filled view. The dead, drifting hulk of our once-great ark hung just outside in the blackness of space.

It must have looked magnificent in its early days. When the cylinders spun and the nuclear reactor engines glowed blue all around it. When the Horizon fleet was the pride of a briefly united Earth, the hope of a doomed planet, ready to carry the lucky few chosen to begin the generations-long voyages to distant planets.

Now it was dead. The giant hole punched by the glancing blow of a stray meteor gaped in its side. That hole was the death knell of the ship, and of nearly everyone left on board.

Fourteen of us were left.

I hugged Shane close, pulling him in front of me, arms wrapped around his shoulders.

Our parents had died on that ship, sucked away into unforgiving space. Nearly everyone we knew, the few that remained even then, had been lost.

We never had time to mourn them. The weight of their deaths pressed on me now, feeling like the cold vacuum of space that took them away. My throat closed around a sob, and I choked it down. *Be strong for Shane.* His shoulders were hitching in my embrace, as he finally felt safe enough to weep for our parents and friends.

A voice murmured from the cuff in my ear.

"It's time."

It wasn't safe to leave the Delta just drifting out there. Even though no one was left alive on it, there were other species that might one day find it. The trajectory of its drift could lead them back to Earth, and it would be centuries before the remnants of human life on Earth were ready to defend themselves from an unfriendly alien visit. The Siitsi would patrol Earth's solar system, but no one in the galaxy knew humans existed. Safer for everyone if it could stay that way a while longer.

A Siitsi male I didn't know stood in the back of the room. The rest of the human crew on the ship were in another viewing area, but this one was just for the Horizon people in this moment.

Six Siitsi shuttles burst from under our window. They circled the dead Horizon in intricate patterns. Shiro had told me it was an honor guard, tracing an ancient pattern in the sky, a remnant of the Siitsi's distant ancestors that once flew on feathered wings in the clear skies of their home world. The ships spiraled around and disappeared back under our feet.

Silent moments passed.

A low, humming growl vibrated through my feet as the grav drive cycled up. Our view changed as the pilots angled us so that the Delta was between us and a blinding white star in the distance. The viewing window darkened until the white sun was a fiery glow, Horizon's silhouette just a small black scar in the middle.

From behind me, the Siitsi began to sing.

His voice was deep and resonant, and in my ear the cuff translated the words he whistled.

Fly you now on silent wings,
As your feathers we enshroud.
Soar away from worldly things,
To a place of silver clouds.

The melody of the Siitsi lament was haunting, and I pulled the cuff from my ear, not wanting to mar the beauty of the song with the robotic, translated voice.

I tipped forward as the grav drive kicked in, pushing us away from the Horizon. It bucked in the sky as the force of the gravity wave hit it, and we watched it grow smaller and smaller in our vision. When the dead ship dove into the white sun, a small, bright plume escaped its surface.

"Goodbye, Mom," I whispered. "Goodbye, Dad."

All around the room, the handful of survivors wept, murmuring their goodbyes to all the loved ones we had lost.

HORIZON DELTA

The Siitsi's song ended, and the door hissed as he left the room. We crowded together, a small group of crying humans, all that remained of the proud Horizon Delta.

There were so few of us left. So many lost.

But against a million odds, we were here. On this alien ship where others of our kind worked in harmony with a species we never dreamed could exist, we were finally safe.

We broke apart and stood gazing out the window as the ship surged forward.

We had a long way to go.

CHAPTER 33

Our tiny Siitsi shuttle was packed with people. We cruised over a lush green planet. Below, an unbroken carpet of green stretched out as far as I could see. Ahead, a mountain range cut into the bright blue sky.

I gripped the edges of my seat as the shuttle swooped up and over the snowy top of the highest mountain peak. We burst over the crest to reveal a bustle of activity in the valley beneath us. Small buildings dotted the flat ground, and the wind of our passing ruffled what looked like the ripple of some kind of energy field over the whole valley.

Shane had the window seat, and I leaned over his lap to take it all in.

We passed through the energy net and landed on a solid pad of dirt. Through the window I saw a rush of people crossing the field to meet us.

I took a deep breath. "You ready for this?"

Shane grinned at me. "We're home. Our home now."

Our hatchway popped open, and Shiro was the first down the ramp. A man about his age ran up to greet him and they hugged, slapping each other on the backs like little kids.

I stood in front of our people at the top of the ramp. *I should say something. This is a big moment.* But nothing suitably momentous came to mind.

"Everybody ready?" I asked and got a bunch of nervous nods.

The ramp bowed beneath us as we trooped down. A warm, fresh smell hit my nostrils, and I breathed in, sucking the hot wind. It smelled a little like the interior of the Botanist's ship. Plants. Growing things everywhere, and a faint, sour tinge I didn't recognize. I held Shane's hand and our feet touched the hard-packed earth together.

"Welcome," said the man who still had an arm around Shiro's shoulder. "Welcome to Carthage."

I moved out onto the landing pad, making room for the people behind me to take their first steps on solid ground. The sound of all them sniffing the air made me smile. I raised my chin a little. *Their first time on a planet.* The thought made me chuckle. *Jonah Campbell, galaxy traveler.*

Shiro brought the man over to Shane and me. His skin was brown, and the edges of his eyes crinkled when he smiled at us.

"Guys, this is Caleb Wilde. He runs the colony here. Caleb, this is Jonah and Shane from Horizon Delta."

Caleb grinned at us. "I've heard bits and pieces of your story from the Siitsi. Can't wait to hear it straight from you." He met my gaze for a moment. "You sound like my kind of kid."

We fanned out behind him, heading for a wide, flat plateau on the side of a cliff. The dark mouth of a cave opened behind it. He pointed out the sights we were passing.

"These are our fields and orchards." He pointed to rows of trees behind us. "Most of those fruit trees were planted by the Siitsi who lived here a couple hundred years ago. I expect you'll find the fruit familiar from your trip."

Siitsi and humans bustled around the fields. Some of the equipment they were using to till the soil looked like scraps of metal salvaged from a wreck. Other things looked bright and new, obviously Siitsi technology.

"We all live here together," Caleb continued. "It's a joint colony, first of its kind. With their help, we've been starting to expand beyond this valley into the mountains all around, so there's plenty of room for all of us."

We passed a wooden corral where a bunch of waist-high creatures scrabbled in the dirt. I stopped and stared at them. They were little, but there was no mistaking what they were.

"You keep dinosaurs as pets?"

Shane rushed to the fence, laughing and pointing.

Shiro nodded. "One of our people domesticated them a while back. They're not pets, but they're great egg-layers. And very tasty."

The Siitsi crew of our shuttle squawked a protest. They didn't eat meat of any kind, but apparently the humans here did.

Caleb turned to Shiro. "Oh, hey, did you get the seeds you were hoping for?"

"Better than seeds." Shiro glanced back at our parked shuttle. "We started germinating them on the trip out here. They grow like crazy."

A shrieking cry above made all of us wince and duck as a huge triangular shape soared over the shimmering energy net far above our heads. The call sent a shiver down my spine. *Dinosaurs. This is a planet of dinosaurs.*

Shane did not share my fear. He had climbed over the corral fence and grabbed one of the little ones, which struggled in his grasp. "Jonah, look! He likes me!"

I laughed. Shane would do just fine here.

Caleb called to some of his people. "Hey, let's get those crates off the shuttle and start planting on the north outer wall. Keep some back inside in case they don't grow well on the slopes."

I remembered Shiro on the day he had found me caked with algae, huddling in a cage on the trade world a million years ago. I had asked him what he was trading for with the Botanists.

Dinosaur repellent.

They had created a plant that the dinosaurs here would hate. He hoped it would keep a bunch of tiny ones he called "The Flood" from trying to get through the mountains every year.

I looked back at my people spread out behind me. They were peering around in speechless shock. I had been through so much since our days on the Botanist ship . . . This green valley was the safest place I could have hoped for. Bright sun beat on the back of my neck, and sweat rolled down between my shoulder blades. It would take some getting used to, this life we should never have had.

A woman took the squirming dinosaur from Shane's grasp and shooed him back to our group. We continued our trek across the field and up a steep slope onto the plateau.

"Welcome," Caleb repeated once we were all assembled. Shiro stood next to him and they faced us with their backs to the valley. We all looked out over this place that would be our new home. "Welcome to Carthage valley." He waved an arm, indicating the huge, green landscape. "We're so happy to have you join our colony. We've been here over twenty years now, and we've got most of the bugs worked out."

I smiled at that. Shiro and the crew had offered to take us to the other planet where the Horizon Beta people lived with the insects they adored. But I had seen what the pheromone could do. Even if it didn't work on humans and bugs the way it worked on Botanists, I'd take dinosaurs over mind-control bugs any day.

"There's plenty of room, and we have quarters already set up for you. Our people will get you settled." He paused. "No, not 'our people.' Your people. All of our people. The descendants of Earth are together again, along with the new friends we've made along the way."

Shiro and Caleb ushered everyone into the caves where I'd been told we would live, and Shane went in with Tishi, the Siitsi female that had taken him under her wing on the three-month voyage here.

I stood outside on the plateau as the sun dipped below the mountaintop, throwing long shadows across the valley that was my home now.

Home.

It was a word as alien to me as the birdpeople that fluttered around the land. Horizon Delta had been my home, the only one I thought I'd ever know. The air here was sweet and fresh, and the noises all around were happy, laughing voices, chirps, and whistles. Everyone seemed content. Shane was safe. He could grow up here without fear and find a place in this budding society.

But as the sky darkened and the first stars appeared in the purple dusk above me, I knew I wouldn't stay here. This wasn't my place. The people here weren't my people. I was born on a spaceship, and that's where I was supposed to die. My life was meant to be spent in the blackness of the night sky, with stars as my companions.

As night on the dinosaur world fell, I realized that one day I would leave this place. When Shane was grown enough not to need me, I'd board another Siitsi shuttle. I'd fly away into that sky, toward whatever adventures waited in the far corners of the galaxy. One day there would once again be a spaceship captained by a human, speeding for a distant world.

I might never make it back to Earth. I might never see Chara d, where the people of Horizon Delta were meant to go.

But my destiny was not here on this warm, green planet.

My destiny was in the stars. And one day I would find it.

"Jonah, you coming?" My little brother's voice echoed in the mouth of the cave. He was silhouetted against the brightness inside.

With one long glance at the darkening night sky, I took his hand and walked into warm light and laughter.

If you love
Horizon Delta

Don't miss D. W. Vogel's *The Forgotten King*
from the *Super Dungeon Series*

Get the book now!
https://www.futurehousepublishing.com/books/the-
forgotten-king/

NEVER MISS A FUTURE HOUSE RELEASE

Sign up for the Future House Publishing email list:
https://www.futurehousepublishing.com/send-free-book/

CONNECT WITH FUTURE HOUSE PUBLISHING

www.facebook.com/FutureHousePublishing

twitter.com/FutureHousePub

www.youtube.com/FutureHousePublishing

www.instagram.com/FutureHousePublishing

ACKNOWLEDGMENTS

It's hard to believe the *Horizon Arc* series is done. These three ships and the people they carried have been a huge part of my life for the past seven years, since I first envisioned a planet of dinosaurs and the ticking clock of dwindling power. Without the support of my village, it would never have come to be.

Deepest thanks to my husband, for enduring the lonely times of being an author's spouse.

To my Future House family: Emma, Stephanie, Olivia, Abigail, Abby, and Adam, for believing in my worlds.

To my agent, Alice Speilburg, who is always in my corner.

To my science guy, Joe, who finds me the answers.

To my faithful readers Nik and Jude, who are always the first to see a new world.

To my friends at Cincinnati Fiction Writers, who let me sit in the front and pretend that the things I say are wise.

And most of all, to the many fans who have come along on this whole journey. We've seen some things together, haven't we? Let's go find some more.

Our destiny is in the stars.

ABOUT THE AUTHOR

D. W. Vogel is a veterinarian, marathon runner, cancer survivor, boardgame developer for SolarFlare Games, and current president of Cincinnati Fiction Writers. She is the author of the *Horizon Arc* series and *Super Dungeon: The Forgotten King* from Future House Publishing.

Connect with D. W. Vogel:
Website: https://wendyvogelbooks.com/
Twitter: https://twitter.com/drwendyv

WANT D. W. VOGEL TO COME TO YOUR SCHOOL?

What makes a hero? Wendy has visited schools and museums to talk with kids about just that. Using *Star Wars* as an example, she takes a look at the classic Hero's Journey in literature. Ideal for grades 3–6, this is a fun introduction into the interpretation of story structure. Through the journey of Luke Skywalker, students will learn about courage, motivation, and the altruism that defines a real hero.

For more information visit:
http://www.futurehousepublishing.com/authors/d-w-vogel/
Or contact: schools@futurehousepublishing.com

CPSIA information can be obtained
at www.ICGtesting.com
Printed in the USA
JSHW042304120920
7828JS00003B/4